Aurel Dobre

The School of Miraveda

LETRAS

Descriere CIP a Bibliotecii Naționale a României
DOBRE, AUREL
The School of Miraveda / Aurel Dobre
—Snagov: Letras, 2023
ISBN 978-630-312-058-4

821.135.1

ISBN eBook ePub: 978-630-312-059-1

English translation made by Cezar Florea

All responsibility for the contents of this book belongs to the author. Copyright 2023, Dobre Aurel.
This book is protected by copyright law.

Distributed by www.piatadecarte.net
Publisher contact: office@piatadecarte.com.ro
Orders at: +40 21 367 5228 // +40 787 708 844

You can contact the publisher for publication requests,
by email: edituraletras@piatadecarte.com.ro
Letras Publishing House / www.letras.ro
contact@letras.ro

Table of content

Table of content....................3
Preface....................5
Chapter 1....................7
Chapter 2....................18
Chapter 3....................35
Chapter 4....................46
Chapter 5....................60
Chapter 6....................73
Chapter 7....................89
Chapter 8....................102
Chapter 9....................114
Chapter 10....................126
Chapter 11....................140
Chapter 12....................149
Chapter 13....................159
Chapter 14....................169
Chapter 15....................178
Chapter 16....................189
Chapter 17....................200
Chapter 18....................210
Chapter 19....................219
Chapter 20....................229

Preface

Reading the book with natural attention, I could remark both the details realism and the ineffable harmony where these are interweaving with the visionary epical episodes, forming a style which certifies the prolific talent of the author.

Concretely speaking about originality and literary value, I had the sensation that the universe of Miraveda has resonances with "Macondo" from Gabriel García Márquez's "One Hundred Years of Solitude".

The value of the book message, toward universality, is protected also by the author's care to minimally link the little universe of Miraveda with time, space, philosophy or politics.

Perhaps, the voice of the novel represents its most original component, which, in this case, not only makes you feel the emotion that transcends the time and the space through all epical episodes, but also makes you to thrillingly read page after page.

—VICTOR GREU

Chapter 1

Ever since he had first seen Codrus, several weeks earlier, Elaur had instinctively read the danger in his stinging gaze, keeping in mind his glassy blue eyes and the rictus that contorted his mouth. His fear had materialized faster than he had thought, as he punched him awfully in the back, after less than two weeks, just for the guilt of trying to avoid him.

After that, he hadn't seen him again at school, he reappeared just now when he was late and the school street was quite deserted. He had seen him quite late, beyond the intersection between them, talking to Basamac, but he hoped he would turn right on his street without being aware of his presence.

Codrus, who had already noticed him, immediately rushed towards him, crossing the street in a diagonal, also determining Elaur to run away. When he had a few more meters to catch him, the first strange thing happened. Although the road was quite flat, Codrus stumbled over an unseen thing, made an unnatural leap through the air and collapsed like a heavy sack, scratching his palms and probably knees exactly when he was reaching his highest speed, that would have shattered any hope of escape.

Taking advantage of his strange fall, which he had looked frightened and astonished, Elaur continued his run with more fervor, turning on that street, accompanied by his swearing and threats.

After another thirty meters of runninghe looked back at his face that was twitched by hatred. As Codrus was approaching menacingly, a second strange thing happened. A metal gate opened suddenly, as though it was unseen, just in front of the fierce Codrus, making him scream in pain and sit near the fence, astonished and disoriented by the blow he received. After looking back again two or three times, seeing that he had escaped Codrus, he thought that without the intervention of Nion, his older brother, neither the obstruction nor the saving gate would have existed.

He was home in less than five minutes, he went directly to his room, put his bag on the table where he was doing his homework and stood slowly on the square stool in front of it.

After he panted heavily, he took out from the bag the sheets he had received from professor Leacu and put them on the table, his gestures were almost mechanical, as he was failing to forget the terrifying image of Codrus's face.

He changed the new uniform with some doc pants and a long sleeve blouse in the same absent minded manner, as he was breathing heavily in order to calm down then he sat again on the chair, with his elbows on the table and his head between his palms, unable to think of something else. It was only after a few minutes, when his breathing returned to normal, that he went to the summer kitchen, where Martia was just putting the hot polenta on a wooden plate in the middle of the table.

"Good evening, mum!"

"Come on, lad! I was just thinking what was going on that you were late. Go and get your sister at dinner. She's in the corner with the girls!"

Elaur left for the gate, as he was still being pursued by Codrus's face. He opened slightly the door, looked left in the direction of the school and only then he dared to go to the right toward the group of laughing girls.

By the time he returned with Alena, the polenta was cut into slices and three steaming plates of chicken stew were waiting on the table, filling the kitchen with the enticing smell of garlic tomato sauce. Minela, his younger sister, who had been born underweight and was still unnaturally weak, was avoiding to touch the stew, hoping to escape only with a small plate of milk, from the kettle where Martia had made polenta and in which she boiled fresh goat milk.

"My dear Minela! Go on and eat your stew and after that you eat milk! The nurse is going to nag me again because I don't give you food! I prepared this chicken especially for you!"

Alena had graduated eight classes and had enrolled as an apprenticeship for a luxury seamstress, to learn a "clean and good" craft, as her mother liked to tell her. Martia, so eager to see her children living better than she had lived, saw her as a famous seamstress, with customers full of money and crazy about dresses made of expensive materials. Feeling instinctively Elaur's unease, she asked him:

"You, Elaur! What did you do today at school?"

"I took an A at the test and I also have another one from last week, when I went out to the blackboard."

Martia didn't say anything else to him. She was very pleased with him, but she felt something was wrong with her boy. Elaur didn't want to tell her anything about his trouble with Codrus, thinking he would find a way to solve the problem without her finding out.

"Professor Leacu asked me to come to the teachers' room and that's why I was late. He gave me the paper from yesterday, from the literature contest, to restore it. He told me he likes it and wants to send it to the City phase!"

After eating the stew, Martia also put in front of them a bowl of milk, three quarts full so you can add a nice slice of polenta. For their father, who was coming after ten o'clock at night from the factory, she prepared a white bowl of milk in which she dipped a large slice of polenta, then she took it to the metal oven of the stove in the bedroom.

"Tonight I will stay until I am done modifying the work and tomorrow morning I will write it properly, said Elaur leaving for his room.

He took several double sheets from the middle of a booklet and began to rewrite the story from the contest. It was past eleven o'clock at night when he turned off the light and laid on the bed, but the memory of what happened when he left school kept disturbing him.

As he closed his eyes he remembered that cold day in March, a few years earlier, with his uncle's cart in Calavechi, having its rugs removed and being covered with a new blanket, pulled in front of their gate, in the mud that flooded the entire street. He hadn't turned six yet, so Martia's little brother had taken him in his arms and put him in the cart, supported on the back its front crate, also covered with that dark red blanket. On the crate, next to his two grandmothers, was his mother's brother-in-law, who was driving the two horses of the cart.

Confused and scared, he looked to the hardened face of his brother Nion, sitting with his feet toward the crate or to his mother who was crying desperately, hardly supported by two of her sisters. His father was walking along the three sisters who were in the first row of the small mortuary convoy. He was pale and shaggy, holding Alena by the hand and looking lost around him. Elaur, scared of everything that was happening, but especially of his mother's crying, was clutching at his father's look as if it were a lifeline, until two big tears rolled down his cheeks, scaring him even more. At that instant, after a front wheel had passed through a pit, his maternal grandmother, to make sure she didn't fall from the cart, turned slightly to the left, stretched out her right hand and caught him by the shoulder.

As he was suddenly comforted by his grandmother's protective gesture and as he had a selfe-defense reflex, the entire road he only watched Memet, a gypsy from the neighborhood, his brother's classmate and the only one who would dare to walk on the the cold mud with his bare feet. He was walking past the fences on the left side of the street, where the ground had been drying, skipping the small puddles that came out of his way and which extended, under the fences, into people's yards. After each jump he would return immediately to his quiet and somewhat solemn walk, in parallel with his colleague's coffin.

Five and a half years had passed since his brother had been trampled by a truck, out of his fault, but also by a drunken carter's fault. He had clung to his cart and the carter whipped at him, making the boy jump in the middle of the road.

The year of the tragedy that struck Elaur's family then became a kind of year zero for them, with all the events being placed before or after this tragedy.

In the six months that had passed from Nion's funeral until the birth of Mina, the girl Martia was carrying in her wombs, she had not dried the tears from her cheeks, so she become hard to recognize on the street, even by close friends. Throughout this period, her daily discussions with Elaur alleviated her suffering, becoming her secret drug. She would make him tell the same stories with and about Nion, and even recite a poem, one of the three he had learned with his help.

At other times, when they had finished the chores, they would both sit on the edge of the bed, holding on their knees the National History of the fourth grade, which remained from him. She would turn the pages of the book and Elaur would shout, breathlessly, the names of historical personalities, represented in dozens of pictures in the book, as he had learned from Nion. Intrigued, however, he watched the tears streaming from his mother's eyes, burning her cheeks and filling her chin, not understanding why he kept repeating this story, if it caused her so much suffering.

Less than a month after the tragic event, he doesn't even know how, Nion appeared in his room, telling him that he would take care of him and help him with anything, but he had to take care of their mother. He did not quite understand how he would take care of his mother, but he trusted Nion, who not only was five years older than him, but until eleven had proven to be a very good, intelligent and obedient boy, appreciated at school and of much help for his parents. For a start, Nion helped him repair his bus which was made from colored boards, with figures of people painted between the windows, which had been brought by Santa and which he had opened to see what was inside.

It was harder when his mother caught him talking to Nion, and he instructed him not to tell her who he was talking to. Only then did he realize that only he could see Nion and even talk to him. Another time, when she had heard him from the other room and asked him what was going on, he said:

"I miss Nion and I pretend to talk to him!"

His mother stared at him as tears were streaming down his cheek and he even heard her the next day when she told his father:

"This boy scares me terribly! I have heard him talk to Nion several times! God forbid, he must not get sick!"

From then on he was careful to close the door and turn his back, whispering, whenever Nion appeared.

One night, when he had gone to the garden to take some radishes, he saw a woman dressed in black who was staring at him, somewhere between the two apricots near the fence. He returned immediately and ran to the door of the house, but he stumbled over something, falling on his belly. When he turned his face up, the woman in black was standing there staring, slightly bent over him. He winced terribly and wanted to scream for help, but the sounds refused to come out of his mouth, as it was clenched with fear.

"Elaur, you had a bad dream, lad! Calm down... your mother is with you!"

Opening his eyes, he saw Martia, who was lying in bed beside him, with tears in her eyes, twisting some wool in the dim light of the oil lamp, which she had taken from the nail in the wall and placed it on the edge of the window that faced the marquise. He had closed his eyes but the nightmare's strong impression did not allow him to fall asleep, and his mother's crying, renewed shortly after that, scared him even harder.

"Come on, mom! Please stop crying! If you cry, Nion will cry too. He doesn't want you to cry!"

Martia stopped crying, looked at him with fear and said:

"What are you saying there, lad? Where did you get those words from?"

As he was sleepy, he almost told her that Nion was telling him those words all the time. Suddenly, the oil lamp, sitting on the narrow, slightly inclined edge of the window, flipped over the blanket on the bed. Rolling over, the glass and the metal cap through which the wick passes were detached from the neck of the lamp and all the oil in the lamp was scattered on half of the bed, immediately bursting into flames from the burning wick. His mother jumped scared out of bed, running to the kitchen, to bring the bucket where they were holding drinking water, when Nion appeared, in a determined voice, telling Elaur to take the pillow and extinguish the fire with it. He was immediately able to put the pillow on the burning blanket and also at Nion's command, he moved it to another burning area. By the time his mother came with the bucket of water, he had almost completely quenched the flames, and they quickly picked up the smoking blanket together and pulled it out onto the sidewalk, where they completely extinguished the fire with water from the bucket.

"Oh, Lord, what a misfortune for us! How wise of you to extinguish the fire with the pillow! Oh, God, we could have gone through a terrible misery!"

She brought another lamp from the hall, slightly increased the flame and put it on the nail in the wall. After shaking the mattress well, she sat down on the bed and, clutching Elaur near her, began to pray:

"Defend, my Lord, the house and the children of fire and water!"

He would have liked to make her happy by telling her that Nion was actually the one who had taught him what to do, but he felt that this would not do her any good. After a few minutes, at his mother's urging, he went to the next room, where he fell asleep right next to his sister, Alena, who was sleeping in peace, without knowing what they had gone through.

Nion hadn't appeared in two or three years, but recalling the obstacles in Codrus's path, he was convinced that only he could save him from his mad rage. He would have liked to see him again, but he immediately thought that he might have already passed that time and he had intervened in this unseen way, just to save him. He fell asleep late, after somehow managing to get off his mind the story with Codrus.

The next morning, before getting out of bed, Codrus's mad face came to his mind and he thought that after what had happened, he hated him even more. He didn't know how he could get to school and especially, how he could get out of there, after sunset, without running into him or any of his comrades.

Without eating, he began editing the story, filling a little over nine pages, on the sheets received from Professor Leacu. He quickly did his math homework, arranged everything in the imitation leather map and only then went to the kitchen. After eating a new portion of stew with a slice of bread, he got dressed and left for school, an hour earlier than usual. At the thirty minutes requested by the literature teacher, he had added thirty more, hoping he would get to school before Codrus.

Moreover, with a street before school, he went to the left and then to the right on a parallel street, the latter one intersecting the school street much closer to the students' entrance. At the intersection, glued to the fence near which he had come, he only moved his head a little, to investigate the street and a piece of the school yard, where the students' entrance was and seeing that there was no danger, he left quickly, stopping just in front of the teachers' room, where Professor Leacu also appeared after a few minutes:

"What happened to you? You came an hour earlier! Just wait for me!"

He entered the teachers' room and in a few seconds he returned with a cardboard map, beckoning Elaur to follow him and after a few steps he stopped at the first window to the school yard and told him:

"Now you can give me the papers! Let's see what came out!"

Elaur carefully removed the papers, with the school stamp applied on the upper left corner, five were written and five were white, he handed them to the teacher, who first counted them, and then carefully read the written ones.

After placing them in the cardboard map, to which he fastened the two small cloth laces attached to the covers, he continued:

"Now it went well! I wanted to help you! You're a little scattered, but I liked your story! Take care! Don't talk to anyone about this! Alright?"

Elaur wanted to tell him about the incident with Codrus, but his stern face and cold, slightly bored look did not encourage him at all. The teacher left for the teachers' room and Elaur, drawing a book from the map, headed to the school library, the one that was full of great promises and surprises. He was determined to look for a much better book than the one he was about to return.

Chapter 2

Tramian had kept his eyes on Martia since the day he saw her, and for a few days he struggled to be as close to her as he tried to get her attention. She glared at him stealthily, then she looked away amused as he tried to catch her attention. She was laughing heartily at the jokes of her friends, watching him as he wasn't able to take his eyes off her, to the annoyance and even the stubbornness of the brigadier, their boss, who had also fallen for her. Struggling to win favor with her, both Tramian and the brigadier, ten years older than them, an old bachelor at thirty-two, shaved daily and dressed more and more carefully, maybe they would melt the heart of the girl from Calavechi.

As that morning he was dressed in blue jumpsuit pants and a pink and blue checkered shirt, Tramian seemed to Martia more handsome than ever. His gaze was seemingly indifferent, so as to cover the grief caused by the brigadier, who was still against him and was sending him to the headquarters of the farm, arranged in the mansion of the former landowner, where he was to enter another brigade. It had been only five days since she had learned from her aunt that they needed people to pick corn at the farm, and she decided to come daily, knowing that jobs were extremely rare and almost exclusively for men. The next morning, she was the first one to arrive at the road leading to the City, from where, with a wagon driven by one of her cousins, together with two other girls from Calavechi and their aunt, they headed for the farm. As it was about an hour's walk away, the farm had been established by the New Authority one year earlier, on the land of an important owner, who was sent to cut reeds in the Delta after a mock trial and his family went to some relatives in the Capital, caring only what he could take in two or three suitcases.

Until lunch break no one managed to get underneath Martia, neither the aunt who loved her like her daughter, nor the girls from Calavechi who had already noticed their gazing game, let alone the brigadier with his crush.

They had lunch, bean with some traces of pork bacon in it, brought from the canteen with a cart drawn by an old and skinny horse, in two large tin plates and served in grey trays of aluminum, exactly on the narrow, sun-burned meadow, from the end of the cornfield. After lunch Martia and three other girls, that were the same age with her, were announced that they had to go to another brigadier, in a place about three kilometers away, called Gradiştea Lupului (*The Wolf's Hill*). They took their little bundles where they kept their spare clothes, the sandals and a bottle of drinking water and left reluctantly to the indicated place. The brigadier, upset by the decision made by the head of the farm, who came on purpose with the chariot, shouted at them:

"Come on, girls! Move faster! Maybe you can be there by nightfall!"

They walked in silence for several hundred meters, striving not to burst into laughter until one of them, winking at Martia, said:

"You're so lucky, girl, as the brigadier likes you! Do you realize? If you had wanted him, you would have made him happy and also help him get rid of his mother's nagging!"

"I have also noticed that he won't take his eyes off me. But what the heck am I supposed to do with him? Is my father dead and I need another father?"

After less than half an hour, they arrived at Gradiştea Lupului, where the new brigadier, a gentle and wise man in his fifties, welcomes them:

"Welcome, girls! Come on! The team entered the field fifteen minutes ago. If you hurry you can catch them immediately."

From the two-meter high corn the front ones were hardly visible, but they could be heard talking, even giggling from time to time. They chose one row of corn, of the four remaining for them and they began to open the big cobs from the husks, to break and to throw them into the piles formed directly on the ground by those in front of them.

At one point, when they began to see the people in front, their buzzing ceased, and everyone's ears caught a song that was already heard. A beautiful voice, of a young man, was heard more and more clearly and the girls who were approaching from behind were not able to see the singer. It was a sweet and a little sad love song which made Martia's heart flutter.

"That was the moment I fell in love with your father! He sang so beautifully, it melted my heart," she said to Elaur, who was listening to her fascinated, seeing that event with his mind's eyes, at his eleven years, as if it was inspired by a love story. After a few moments, as Martia saw her son's expectation, continued:

"I had no thoughts of marriage. My father had died two years earlier, my mother was ill and we were poor. What dowry could mom give us? Your grandfather had given all the blankets, the rugs and the quilts, woven or stitched with great difficulty, plus the best clothes, for five sacks of flour and six of corn, so that we could go through the famine of forty-seven. Out of desperation, more men left the village, all the way to the region where the Great River enters the country, where the drought had been less harsh, with carts full of dowry things and returning with flour and corn, which, normally, were not even worth a quarter of the things given in exchange. Two weeks to the destination and two in return, they traveled hundreds of kilometers, sleeping only three or four hours during the day, in the shade of some tree, to travel more in the cold. They walked by the carts to spare their horses, as they were hungry too, because they didn't even find grass on the road. Poor dad got pneumonia, which lead to his death a few weeks after returning.
He was going among strangers and we were crying at home together with your grandmother after our lost dowry. Although he was ill, he told us when he returned: "Daddy's girls, your life is more important than that dowry! We can also pass this test and in two or three years we can get the dowry back." But, as those people came and took our land, our hopes were destroyed and it was even worse that our father died! He paid with his life, so we could go on.

"Hey, lad! You could write an entire book about how much we suffered and there would still be some things left to tell. But let's get back to our business, as they say!

I met your father in September, I went out with him a few times for a walk, and at the beginning of November, when the work at the farm was done, I stayed home, in Calavechi, and he went to work at a new factory, all the way next to Ciuntița train station. By the end of April he sent me a message through my cousin, who had also been hired there, to meet the next Saturday, to go to a movie in the City."

"I met him, we went to the movie and after that he told me that he had thought it over and he wanted to marry me and run away together. He had a job from then on and during those times it was a big deal. As I had been thinking all winter only about him, I decided immediately to run away with him that night."

"What do you mean to run away with him?" Elaur asked innocently.

"Oh, yes, we ran away! We left for their house in Miraveda and immediately it started to rain cats and dogs. We ran like two crazy people, laughing and holding our hands, through that rain, which had wet us to the skin! The next day, on Sunday, he borrowed a bicycle from a neighbor, and we both went to my mother in Calavechi, who knew nothing about me, the poor thing. Like any mother, she had a feeling, knowing that I went to meet the boy from Miraveda, but she was still holding her breath, thinking that something bad might have happened to me. When we got there, we explained her the situation, I gathered my things in a big basket, she also put for me two homemade breads in a smaller basket, a piece of cheese and two bottles of milk from a poor cow, which my father had been stubborn to pass through the drought, we kissed and that was it."

"You didn't tell me what this runaway was like," Elaur said, especially to provoke her to continue her story.

"Well... my boy, when two young people got together without asking their parents' permission, they were they run were accused of running away. They would go to the boy's house or to some of his relatives and that was it! Even if the girl's parents, or even the boy's, were upset, there wasn't much they could do. So the boy and especially the girl were considered married and they remained like that. After a while they went and did their papers at the town hall and the family was ready."

"We were poor, my boy", Martia continued. "Even the dress I was wearing while meeting your dad had been borrowed from a friend, but he didn't want me to give it back. 'I took in it, so you keep it! I will pay for it when I get my salary' and that's what he did. He paid for it at the first salary and at the next one he bought me a pair of white sandals, a blouse and a pleated skirt, making me very proud of my man.

***

For most, Miraveda was just a village of farmers and fishermen, set up at the end of the previous century on the five or six meter high bank, where the swollen waters of the Great River often stopped. In the meantime, becoming the City's district, Miraveda remained the same village flooded with greenery, with dirt roads, no running water or sewage, with hot summers and suffocated in winter by the snows brought by the harsh wind from the east. It was, however, the almost perfect place for a happy childhood, with all its dust or mud, or maybe exactly because of all of those. The village had been designed on both sides of the national road that connected the City to the Capital, a hundred and twenty kilometers away, passing through dozens of villages. Established especially for the peasants that owned land in the area, by royal decree, it had been well designed, with straight and long streets, parallel to the road, at the same distance from each other, surrounded by slightly shorter perpendicular streets, also located at equal distances that resulted in twenty identical plots of land, on each side of the street, between two short streets.

The lots on one street, with an opening of twelve meters and a depth of fifty meters, corresponded to identical lots with opening on the other street, all having six hundred square meters. The parallel streets, interspersed with perpendicular streets, formed an almost perfect rectangular system, so as to definitively determine Elaur's spatial perception, which often helped him in his life, but also confused him, when he had to find an address in a city with twisted streets.

The surface area of six hundred square meters was designed to be enough for a house with three or four rooms, kennels and animal shelter in line with the house, but also a flower garden and a vegetable garden for family consumption. Most of the newcomers have been appropriated or they bought two lots, to keep room for some nice vineyard, seven to eight fruit trees for the joy of the children and also a larger yard for raising birds. Most courtyards, bounded on the street by fences of whitewashed planks, had smaller fences between them, from grooves or even from sunflower-dried sticks. At the beginning of the village most of the properties became slowly small farms where you could find dozens of chickens, two or three pigs, as well as a cow or a goat for milk.

Tramian's father, born in Miraveda, had gotten married when he was twenty-three years old, just two weeks after returning from the war, with the girl who had been waiting for him faithfully for three years. His chosen one was from Miraveda, but she had been born in the neighboring county, in a lost village in the plain from the north of the Capital, from where she had come with her family when she was just a child, following a relative of theirs, who had made a small fortune in the area from selling salt and dried fish. Martia's mother was born in Calavechi, but her father moved to that village when he was around eight years old, from a village in the north of the county, around forty kilometers away, together with his mother and another brother and three sisters, in order to claim the five acres plot of land received as widows and orphans of war. Coming from families impoverished by war and hunger, both left without a father, Tramian and Martia each had a nice genetic mix, having beautiful faces and bodies and they were also quite smart. They hadn't been doing great in school, having only four classes each, which were also finished with great difficulty because of all kinds of shortcomings. Their marriage started right from the spoon and the fork, all their belongings could be kept in a wooden suitcase, with which Tramian had been in the army, and in two or three rush baskets.

"We stayed for three weeks at your grandmother, where your father's sister was living, with her husband and their first boy. We could have had a room for us, we could also have built a house in the yard, but your grandmother told us that your father had a salary and he had to deal with the situation. Perhaps it also mattered that both his older brothers had already organized their life, the first in a marginal neighborhood of the City, and the second, paying rent, in the seaside town."

"Your father obeyed his mother's decision and a week after I ran away with him we started looking for a room for rent. We took a shack, my boy! We repaired it for ten days, we straightened the crenellated walls and glued them with yellow clay, I changed the window, from which remained only the wrecked frame, I also made a stove with hob, then I whitewashed everything, so it seemed like it had been new."

After a pause during which Martia looked thoughtfully, remembering those years, she continued:

"In seven years of renting, we changed four hosts, as the owner, after seeing the house repaired, after a few months began to press us that he needed that room and that in the spring we were supposed to go elsewhere. The hardest part was when the third host asked us to move. I had given birth to Nion and Alena, but we had also bought some materials for the house and we carried the children with us and also the plank, the sconces, four doors and three windows. From the first years, the New Authority, installed after the Great War, had forcibly gathered all the arable land of the people in the collective farms and increased the taxes for all the animals in the courtyards. With such taxes and in the absence of food and especially of grain, the number of animals and birds has decreased considerably, people being more and more dependent on what was or was not often found in state stores. However, the fish, which had always been the food of the poor, was abundant in Miraveda, and Martia and Tramian thus found an additional way to supplement the family budget, but especially to save money for the little house they dreamed of.

Every year Tramian waited for the three weeks of rest leave from the factory, not to rest, but to work at the state fishery, improvised under the shore where Miraveda was, where he was doing all kinds of work, the payment being made in fish, at the end of each day. It was hard to find customers for the fish that was not consumed immediately, so Martia cleaned it of its scales, eviscerated it and salted it, putting it dry on the specially stretched peaks then drying it on the specially stretched cords. The dry fish, destined for winter consumption, when the pond and the lake south of Miraveda froze, was moved from November to the attic, spread on the specially placed cords, becoming the small food bank of the family.

In heavy winter days, when vegetables disappeared from the garden and also from poor state stores, the only ones allowed to trade, Martia would climb in the attic, descending with two hardened fishes that were opened like the covers of a book, she put them in water overnight, in order to melt the salt. The next day, she had a lot of recipes available for its preparation, from the well-known plate, to the fish boiled with rice and even the fish fried on a hot plate and served with garlic sauce in which could be added some tomato juice to taste. And after moving to their new home, until the pond and the lake near Miraveda were dried by the New Authority, Martia would buy fish every year to salt it and prepare it for the winter. After drying it well, she stored it in a cool cottage, dug in the ground, where they kept sauerkraut and pickles during the winter, using it as a natural refrigerator the rest of the time.

In the first years of marriage, in the beginning with some of the fish that Tramian gained from the fishery and then with fish bought from fishermen from Miraveda, Martia had started a small business, traveling by train, most often alone and when possible with her husband, each of them carrying fifteen to twenty kilograms of fresh fish, in villages fifty to sixty miles away from the Great River, where they were welcomed with open arms, even if here, the fish was not as cheap as in the localities along the Great River. Exactly from this difference in price, eliminating the price of the train transport, the two spouses earned the money to buy their house and some of the materials they needed for the construction.

The representatives of the New Authority were not only unable to organize a normal trade, they also considered these small actions of private trade as speculation, Martia risking not only the confiscation of the fish, but also stinging fines. Only their appearance of honest and hardworking people kept them safe from the zealous and merciless vigilance of the control bodies installed in the stations.

A few years later Elaur heard his mother talking with her older brother, Gicu, who was a captain in the army:

"What was my crime, brother? We bought fish from Miraveda, the next day we woke up at dawn, pulling fish baskets to the station, buying tickets and going to the respective stop, descending and pulling heavy baskets to the village. We sold the fish at the local price, which was higher than the one in Miraveda, but if it wasn't, why would I have struggled so much? What speculation have we done? We didn't set the prices when I bought it, not even when we were selling it, because everyone knew about the prices. After selling the fish, there were even people who were upset that they didn't buy, so they asked us to come the next week."

Gicu, looking at her sympathetically, said:

"Good thing you didn't have to deal with them. They were able to investigate their own mother!"

"Well, one evening, they even caught us on the train with four rush baskets full of fish. They got us off the train at the first bigger station, took us to an empty room, and kept us there almost all night. There were only three baskets left, the fourth one being left in the train wagon and seeing that the turn had changed and the people who came did not know how full the baskets had been, under the pretext that he had a stomach upset, Tramian went many times to the latrine in the yard. We didn't know what they could do to us, but he was afraid that he would lose his job so each time he went to the latrine he would put two big fish between his shirt and his skin, which he would then throw in the pit of the latrine. By morning, in the three baskets were left about fifteen pounds of fish from sixty pounds."

As she was looking at her brother who was amused, she continued:

"If they were so smart and they were on people's side, why didn't they trade fish? They had the fish and the money, plus all the cars and the trains were on their hands. After all, we were not grabbing money from anybody and people were expecting us to be happily especially before the holidays when they were allowed to eat fish."

Martia and Tramian bought the doors and the windows from the earnings, as well as other construction materials, the savings being put aside for the purchase of the land. After six hard years of collecting money, Martia laid her eyes on a building plot made of two lots and after two weeks they were certified owners. They spent all the money they had raised for the building plot, plus a small loan from Tramian's brother, so they waited another year until they started to build it. Instead, they had bought most of the building materials as the widespread shortage of goods was prompting people to buy the materials when they found them and not when they needed them.

The following year, for three months, they kept making clay and straw bricks up to the number they knew from the mason, for a three-bedroom house and an anteroom, as Martia had seen at a friend of hers in the City. The black soil was taken from a pit dug in the back of the yard and the bricks were made right there, near that pit. On the first evening, Tramian dug a row of earth with the spade, throwing the earth with a shovel beyond the edge of the pit, from where Martia drew it with her dig, placing it in the form of a circle, with a large hole in the middle, where she was going to pour water.

The next evening, when Tramian returned from the factory, they began to carry two buckets of water each, the water taken by Martia during the day from the well and put in two metal barrels, in the sun. After filling the void in the earth ring, they began to lift the earth from the edges with shovels and throw it in the middle until all the earth was soaked, obtaining an earth stack, as it was called in Miraveda. Martia would take a good amount of straws and walk barefooted into the warm earth stack that was reaching to her knees and she would spread straws evenly and step on them energetically to mix them with the moist soil. Tramian would shovel the edges of the stack for a while throwing the wet, hard clay to the center, where Martia added some straws and stepped back on it. Towards the end, Tramian also entered near Martia and holding each other they continued that dance almost ritually, until Martia decreed, resolutely:

For a time, Tramian shoveled the edges of the tip, throwing the damp, hard ground toward the center, where Martia added some straw and stepped back again. Towards the end, Tramian also entered near Martia and holding each other, that dance continued almost ritually, until Martia decreed, resolutely:

"Alright! We're good! That's enough for today!"

They would go near the two barrels and after pouring water for each other with a clay jug, until they were thoroughly cleaned of the soil, at the end they would wash with the warm, clean water from a clean basin. They would also drink a few jugs of cold water recently taken from the well and soaked with effort they would leave and take their children from Tramian's mother, they would eat what they could find and sleep with the children.

They went near the two barrels and after pouring water on each other with a clay jug, until they were thoroughly cleaned of the soil, at the end, they were washed in warm, warm water from a clean basin.

"At four o'clock in the morning your grandmother would come and stay with you three, because you had been born for a year and I and your father came here, at the house, to get the job started," she told Elaur. Before leaving for the train station to catch the six-and-twenty-five train with which he was going to the factory, Tramian carried large balls for me from the clay and straw stack, as large as he was able to carry with a big pitchfork, and put them around the place where the bricks were aligned and I was already starting to make them. He would carry three quarters of the stack until he left and I would take the rest by myself when I got the rows of bricks near the stack.

With a good pattern, as the Miraveda people called the wooden template, forty centimeters long, twenty centimeters wide and fifteen centimeters high, Martia tied the large and black bricks on the flat ground, in four or five parallel rows. In the pattern that was washed after each use, in an old basin that she was pulling to be at hand, she thickened the clay and straw balls, pushing them well into the corners, so that the bricks would come out resistant and with full edges. After she smoothed the top of the brick with her palm, she pulled up the wooden handles, fastened to the ends of the pattern, leaving a beautiful brick on the ground. And another one, then another one, up to one hundred and fifty, one hundred and sixty pieces. From time to time she stopped to breathe a little and, looking at the perfectly aligned bricks, she had a feeling of uncontrolled force, daydreaming about their future home.

After two days, they would lift the bricks on the edge, dry them on the lower side, and when they were almost dry, they would place them in a shape of pyramid, with spaces between them, through which the air would circulate, continuing to dry the bricks, but they could also be covered with pieces of asphalted cardboard, to protect them from the rain. Only when they were perfectly dry did they both carry them and put them together, in a large, compact pile, closer to the street, where they would build the house. Then they took care to cover the growing pile again, with asphalted cardboard and tiles from those purchased for the roof, so as not to let their work be ruined by the intense summer rains, which sometimes came unexpectedly.

In July, when the last bricks were dried, Tramian took leave from the factory and, with a skilled craftsman, who was their neighbor, but who was also Martia's brothers neighbor from Calavechi, in a week they raised the walls, they built the wooden structure of the roof and they also placed the tile on the house and from that moment on it could rain as much as possible. For an entire week, side by side with Tramian, Martia nailed the ceiling slabs, between the grooves supported on the walls, from which the entire roof was fixed. The following Sunday, with all of Tramian's annoyance, accustomed since he was a child to respect the day left by God for rest, Martia made a luncheon, which was usually organized with close relatives and some of the neighbors.

Thus, all her relatives from Calavechi could come, plus Tramian's sister, managing to "put clay in the attic" for the entire house, that is, they covered the part of the attic of the structure made of beams and and slats, with clay soaked with water and mixed with straw which, after drying, became the ceiling of the house and was then to be tightened underneath with yellow clay, mixed with wheat bran.

In the following week, assisted by sisters and brothers-in-law, in three days they used the same yellow clay mixed with bran, to replace the plaster, for the whole exterior of the house, ensuring the wall sealant and a slightly more pleasing appearance as well.

Martia stuck on her own all the interior walls, the ceilings and the floors, first with yellow clay with bran and the last finish, according to the tradition, was made with yellow clay mixed with water and horse manure which not only provided a much better finish but the applied layer was gaining strength and was free of cracks.

In the meantime, Tramian had bought five or six bags of lime that he slacked with water, in a not too deep pit, dug near the house. Martia painted all the interior walls with that lime, the perfectly flat ceilings and even the floors, thus solving the aesthetic part and finding the best and most handy disinfection as well. With the same white lime she also covered the three stoves, made of burnt brick and stuck with the same yellow clay. Two of the stoves were provided with hotplates and metal ovens.

At the end of September , the big move came, not before the traditional and proper sanctification, during which Father Baicu, who had known Tramian since he was little, gave them a big icon with the Mother of God with the baby, sanctified and framed very beautifully.

The following Sunday, Martia invited her relatives to a rooster soup with homemade noodles and roast chicken with potatoes in the oven, thus checking one of the stoves with hotplate and oven in the room she had temporarily assigned as a kitchen, until they would raise money to build a kitchen, attached to the house! Tramian had also brought to the table a bottle of plum brandy and five bottles of wine with the corks covered with pitch which he had buried the previous autumn, exactly for this event, somewhere in the yard, in a place only he knew. They continued the party until the evening enjoying their house which still smelled of lime and oil paint but from which no one asked them to move.

Chapter 3

Elaur had few pleasant memories from the first two years of school. He had been enrolled in an experimental class with middle school teachers in arithmetic, music, drawing and physical education. The calligraphy hours were held by an elderly teacher who was also deputy director. A teacher had been appointed for reading. He was as jaded as he was old and gentle and he also held the place of head teacher.

In the third grade, after the retirement of the old teacher, in his place came a much younger teacher, who had conquered Elaur since the first lessons.

The reading hours were transformed, as if by miracle, into captivating stories, followed by true contests, "who's the first to raise his hand", that is exactly the opposite of the gray moments spent with the old teacher, which kept going monotonously and painfully, until the saving bell rang and broke the cold quiet of the school hall. For her part, the new executive had been surprised by the essays he had written which had brought him three marks of A in just two weeks.

„ I'm mad at you, Elaur! You are a rough diamond," said Mrs. Dida at the next class.

It was the second time he hadn't done his homework and the head teacher's words sounded more like disappointment than scolding. Elaur, who knew how simple were the exercises received as homework, tried to save the situation:

„ But I know how to solve those exercises! You'd better give us an essay!"

„I am the one who gives the homework and they are mandatory for the entire class! The fact that you know how to solve them does not absolve you of guilt. Here's how we do it! I'm not going to ruin your school situation now but if I catch you only once without your homework, you don't get only one F, but two Fs!"

„Maybe, three Fs!" – the new colleague was heard from the last bank, he had repeated the third class and seemed older at least three or four years than the others.

Mrs. Dida, waiting for the few approving laughters that had followed her reply to stop, said in the same calm voice:

„I see you're good at arithmetic! If you were that good at reading we would be talking!"

Neither the prospect of a bad mark, nor the rude jokes from the breaks that followed, with frequent references to the „rough diamond", did not make Elaur as sad, as much as having disappointed Mrs. Dida.

At the reading hour the following day, Mrs. Dida asked as usual:

„Who wants to read the essay you had to write at home?"

Immediately, from the bottom of the class was heard a specially deepened voice, in order not to be recognized:

„The rough diamond!"

Mrs. Dida, serene as always, looked at the pupils then rotated her eyeballs as she did every time she thought about what to propose for home and said:

„Wait! Wait one moment! Here's how we do it! You, Elaur, have to write an essay as school assignment, here in class. As I work with your colleagues, you have to write an essay entitled ‚My Mother'!"

As he was slightly blushing because of the little challenge with which Mrs. Dida wanted to clarify things, he asked permission to use a pencil and an eraser instead of the pen and the ink, as he wasn't too good with those. With the notebook in front and the pencil in his hand, Elaur took a few moments to look out the window, in the direction of their house, where his mother, probably with the food boiling on the stove, was also busy doing other household chores until he felt a pleasant warmth, as if she were behind him, caressing him on the top.

The words that had begun to flood his brain flowed quite easily on the notebook in front of him and only the moments when he used the eraser to delete a word or even a sentence that did not please him took him out of that special state to observe the curious looks of his colleagues, especially the girls' looks.

Mrs. Dida, walking among the benches, glanced from time to time in his notebook and before the recreation she reserved the time needed for Elaur to read aloud what he had written. She sat on her chair with her left hand under the chin, looking almost maternally at Elaur, leaning her head slightly to the left, as if to better hear what he was reading. After he finished reading, he looked up at her, joining the others, who were waiting for Mrs. Dida's verdict, which came after a few long seconds of looking out the window:

„You already have three As! Today I am not giving you a mark, but I am giving you a more special homework!"

After a brief pause in which she looked significantly at the class, she continued with a voice warmer than ever:

„When you get home, ask your mother to sit on a chair and tell her that the homework I gave you is to read this essay! Is that clear?"

From that moment on the malicious jokes ceased but the expression „rough diamond" has been following Elaur for many years, as a secret mantra, preventing him from many moments of relaxation and reminding him of the best head teacher that ever existed.

In the next two years, in which he never disappointed Mrs. Dida, from the mediocre pupil, noted especially for the energy he consumed during breaks, Elaur managed to take the third prize in that year and the second prize in the fourth class. As fortune always favours those who know how to enjoy it, Elaur was pleased to find out that she will be a literature and head teacher even in his first year of middle school.

In the summer before fifth grade, Martia had raised money to prepare Elaur for school. At the beginning of September, together with Elaur, she was already in a row at the children's clothing store, built from wide planks, on the main alley of the Fair organized in the northern part of the city. As it was still early, there were only a few people in front of them, including a friend of hers from Miraveda, who came with her girl, to buy her an uniform and some notebooks for the first grade.

„Well done Martia! Look what a big boy you have! Does he deserve new clothes?"

„Of course he does! He finished the fourth grade with the second prize and Mrs. Dida, when she gave him the prize, told him there on stage, in front of everyone else, that when she leaves the Miraveda school she wants Elaur to take her place. She brought tears to my eyes and I didn't touch the ground until we arrived home!"

Her friend, looking at Elaur with surprise and patting her shoulder, said:

„Is that true, lad? You might become a great gentleman, that you will never recognize us on the street!"

As he was flusterd, the boy couldn't say a word because, as she came in front of the seller, said to Martia:

„Come on, tell him what you want to buy! I am going to look inside, to see what I can buy for my daughter!"

Martia asked for a school uniform, pointing to Elaur, which he, at the saleswoman's suggestion, tried on right there, pulling the blue pants over the short khakis, and the coat over the blue poplin blouse buttoning it up all the way so that it was obvious that a flannel could be worn underneath it. After asking for two white and two blue shirts, some t-shirts and a pair of black sports shorts, she asked the seller to give her a count. The seller, knowing Martia well, pulled out a black coat with a large, blue and purple plaid pattern and said to her:

„Don't you want something like this?"

Martia looked slightly sadly at Elaur thinking she wasn't able to borrow the necessary money and she answered:

„Offf, he is such a beautiful boy! He deserves it but with the money I have I am supposed to buy him a school bag and some notebooks for school!"

„OK, Forget about it! I might keep one for you. It's cheap and the cloth is good. Come at my store after the Fair, at „Two Rabbits". Alright?"

After Martia nodded shaking her head both of them queued at „Our Bookstore" where, after waiting for an hour in a row, Elaur chose a black school bag made of artificial leather, like a briefcase without handles with two zippers that opened on the side, orange-faded, giving it a more cheerful aspect. After he chose the school bag, Martia also asked:

„Five lined notebooks, three with squares, two practice sheets, three pencils, a color box, a list of vocabulary, a ruler, a set square, a compass and a protractor.

After Elaur put what she had bought in his new school bag and Martia paid, she told him:

„That's enough for now! Mum will buy you more during school. Now I'll take you to the carousel. We won't just go home without you enjoying the Fair too!"

For about an hour, Elaur ran from the boats to the carousel and from the carousel to the chains, he climbed those three times in a row, returning to the carousel, where he would only accept to climb the „satellite".

After all this frolic, Martia took him to the stalls that were placed on two rows, where she bought a blue rubber ball, a metallic „referee" whistle, a white-and-blue striped shirt as well as a dark blue cap, with a small yellow anchor embroidered in front. She looked at him happily and in order to get everything right she sat in line at the big donut shop which was spreading its haunting smell all over the Fair, she bought four hot donuts, well coated in powdered sugar mixed with vanilla and two ice juices!

After eating the donuts and refreshing themselves with that lemon-flavored juice, they headed for the exit of the Fair, where Elaur was expected for a new treat. Since the arrival Martia had been watching the popsicle vendor, whom she knew from the Great Market, with his well-known refrigerator on wheels and who had the best ice cream in town.

She bought three ice creams, she gave one of them to a gypsy boy, who was staring at the ice cream box:

„This is for you, lad! Be it for the soul of my boy, Nion!"

After eating the ice cream, Martia bought two more and they left for Miraveda, enjoying them on the path running parallel to the railway. After crossing the *Two Roosters* neighborhood, they carefully crossed the four rails and headed towards the intersection called „The Troublemaker", after the popular name of a disappeared tavern. Not long before, there were even quite a few men who got into trouble, first with a glass and then with several, spending a lot of money from what they had earned at the stockyards, for some pig or for the grain they had sold.

From there, making a right on the road, near the gray and quite high fence of the garrison, then passing the imposing building of the Agricultural High School, after about two hundred meters they reached the Mill, which was just at the entrance to Miraveda.

The beginning of September had begun with summer temperatures and the ice cream, in addition to the cooling sensation, would both enhance their well-being. Elaur was proud, carrying the bag as a well-deserved trophy, while Martia was overwhelmed by a great deal of gratitude that could be guessed easily in the spark of her eyes, but especially in the way she couldn't take her eyes off him.

Five weeks after the start of the fifth grade, when everything seemed to be going very well, ingratiating himself to Mrs. Parvu, the new math teacher, but also to Professor Leacu, who taught literature older kids, there was that event with Codrus, and now he was expecting the worst consequences.

In the last three years, Codrus, Butulan and the youngest of the Basamac brothers inspired real fear for the pupils of the Miraveda school. From drunken and scandalous parents, feared by everyone, the two did not scare Elaur as much as Codrus terrified him, even though he was part of a nice and pretty wealthy family. He had repeated the fifth and sixth classes, and now he repeated, for medical reasons, the seventh grade, he was almost seventeen and even the teachers feared him.

Codrus was afraid only of the physical education teacher Elian, a thirty-five-year-old man, neither very tall nor very athletic, but strong and especially careless. Elaur heard that less than two weeks after the beginning of the fifth grade, one evening, when Codrus and Butulan had sat on the sides of the school exit door, picking the pockets of the younger students and slaping most of them, as they were only guilty of having nothing in their pockets.

On his way out Elaur saw how Lefan, his deskmate, was slapped badly on the back of the head by Butulan and then he turned suddenly climbing back up the stairs to the first floor, where his class was. Provoked by his gesture, Codrus went after him and although he had started to run, before opening the classroom door, he punched him badly between his shoulder blades, throwing him to the ground.

As she opened the door, the math teacher saw Elaur thrown on the floor with Codrus over him, she screamed „Guuuuys!!", trying to impose her authority, although she was afraid of him. Moving indolently, Codrus looked at her frowning, defying her for a short while, then he turned ostentatiously and slowly left.

Mrs Parvu, with a quite visible walking problem, slowly approached Elaur and after asking him if he was okay, fearing that the fella might return, sent a girl through the other end of the hall to the gym on the ground floor to notify the physical education teacher. As professor Elian found out what had happened, he rushed to the pupils' exit but the two punks, seeing him, ran away, leaving the school yard through a hole in the fence and then disappearing on a side street.

To this affront, difficult to accept, had now been added the humiliating fall, as well as the gate that had struck him cruelly, all bound in his mind, by Elaur and only Elaur. The latter was thinking how to get the help of Professor Elian when he received the librarian's consent to enter, putting on the table the book that had to be returned with an almost mechanical gesture. After finding out his name, Miss Alicia began to look for his file, scanning more than half of the files in a plywood box, which had a Roman five written on its end. As she checked the refund, showing him as always the shelf with several books which also had the same Roman five written on a white cardboard glued to the middle of the wooden frame at the top.

He was not so happy that he had to choose the books he borrowed only from the fifth grade shelf, he could hardly find a book to attract him. Thinking of Codrus and how he could present to Professor Elian the last event with him, he was quite absent minded while browsing the used books, lined up on the shelves, when he saw a girl standing between the shelf for the seventh grade and the two shelves for the eighth grade and he beckoned her to him. He walked timidly to her, impressed by her incredibly white face, not daring to look up into her blue eyes. As his heart was pounding with emotion, he tried to understand what she wanted from him. She looked at least two or three years older and her slender body could be seen under a pale green flowing dress over which she wore a dark green tunic with green embroidery on the sleeves and on the side.

„Look! You can borrow this book!" she said, handing him a book with glossy blue-green covers, without any particular illustration, on which she could only read the name of the author, Daniel Defoe. He took the book, grateful that he had escaped the children's books from the shelf for the fifth grade. As he was rather flustered, until he reached the librarian's office he managed to read the book's title, „Robinson Crusoe".

„What have you done, my dear? You've jumped right into the eighth grade" she said, looking carefully over her reading glasses and smiled. However, she completed the name of the book and the author as well as a number written on the first sheet and gave it to him:

„When you return it, I'll check if you've actually read it!"

He picked up the book distracted by the girl's blue and smiling eyes, who followed him amused and was heading for his class on the other end of the floor. He didn't understand who she was, or what was the connection between her and Alicia, the librarian. Only when he got home after the evening meal, opening the book, did he realize what a wonderful book the mysterious and beautifully dressed girl had recommended to him.

Chapter 4

Martia loved Elaur with the despair of the mother who had lost a son and his school results made her daydream. She saw him as a teacher at the Miraveda school or as an officer in the army, like her brother, Gicu. She had only four years of primary schooling, she graduated the school in Calavechi, where she would go every third day, as she was needed in her household, she had learned how to write, but especially how to count and there were only a few that would compete against her.

With his innate tradecraft she knew how to supplement her family's income by going to the Big Square on Sunday morning with radishes, green onions and some garlic from the garden of the house, astonishing the ladies of the city, attracted by her fresh and beautiful merchandise, with the speed and especially with the accuracy of her calculations.

„There you go: radishes, 7 times 0,75 equals 5,25. Onions, five times 0,50 equals 2,50 and garlic, three times 0,60 equals 1,80. In total, 9,55. I'll give you one extra radish, to make it ten!"

With her luminous figure, inspiring confidence, she easily sold the goods on the stool and quickly returned with the money of which she only took a small part to buy three triangular pieces of gingerbread and by the time Tramian came from the church the food was ready and the table was set.

Elaur liked her stories, especially on rainy Sundays, when after lunch she kneaded dough for donuts, letting it to ferment for a while, in the wooden pot, covered with a clean napkin over which she put a fur, to grow faster. When the dough was just fine she would spread it and she woul cut the round donuts with a cup then she would put the in the hot oil, in a large saucepan, frying them on both sides. Sizzling in the hot oil, they were incredibly puffy, resulting in round, almost spherical, donuts which, after taking them aside and allowing them to drain, put them in a porcelain bowl in which she had placed a bag of powdered sugar and two envelopes of vanilla sugar, finally putting them in a glazed bowl, from which everyone was served. When the last donuts were ready, she woud also sit down with the others at the table, watching happily as they were eating her flavored donuts and began to tell:

„When I was a girl, in Calavechi, my mother used to make me donuts and was always proud to make the best donuts in the whole village. On Christmas Eve we didn't sing carols like in Miraveda. The village was divided into two equal parts and the the carol singers into two large cohorts, one for each half of the village. The cohort who was singing around our part of the village was taking a break at our house because there were four girls in the house and also because your grandfather was waiting for them with the glasses filled with red wine and the girls with a big pot full of hot donuts. We had a good life, lad, because we were all working both the family land and alo „partly" at the boyar, twice more. We had enough flour, corn for the animals and also for dough, ten or fifteen sheep, three cows, two or three pigs, but there were also nine mouths to feed. Your grandfather had a really kind soul but may heavens protect you if he caught you with lies or being lazy. If you didn't work, not only did you not eat, but he would take care of you and after my father punished you, you would lose any desire to do something like that! In addition to the Christmas pig and the Easter lamb, which were established in our tradition, he would also cut a pig during the year which we used to make meats and sausages and also fat meat roasted in the oven. He would also cut some barren sheep of which he made *floe* or, if it was spring, pastrami and sausages, which were put to dry in the eave."

„What did you mean he made *floe*? He was putting it in the ice?" Elaur asked curiously.

„No, my boys! That was its name, *floe*! But it wasn't frozen. The sheep meat was boiled with spices and two or three sliced onions until it fell from the bones and there was also some gravy. That meat was strongly boiled and spiced. He divided it in two or three pots over which he poured some hot gravy and then he would put it in the cold pantry. After it cooled down, the meat and the juice were curdled and it looked like a slab of ice which is why it was called like that. We cut slices of it with a knife and ate it with baked bread or hot polenta and we were healthy, my boy!"

After a short break, during which she also ate a donut, she continued:

„Twice a week, your grandmother would curdle milk in five or six clay pots which she put in the cold pantry. After two or three days we gathered the cream from above which, sometimes we would stir until our hand hurt to make butter. Besides what we ate, your grandfather had enough customers in the City for cream, butter or even entire pots. Curdled milk, which was good for the stomach, was also a cure for headache after a drink. I remember how he put the horses at the carriage and left on the road on the border and then on the Trestichii Valley to the City, where he was expected with curdled milk, thick cream that could be cut with a knife, bread baked in the oven and even a prepared sheep, then fresh eggs, some fat rooster or duck. He wasn't going to the market! He had his customers in the City and he never left with unsold merchandise. He would return in the evening after buying salt, sugar, spices, some oil and a can of gas for the lamp and also ginger bread, a box of halva or Turkish candy cane. He would get angry easily but still had a good soul and he loved the seven of us. He was really proud of his children when he was meeting with friends over a beer on Sunday in the village inn or when they were leaving with seven or eight carts at the fair in the City to sell what they had: wheat, corn, a pig, a calf or other animals. One winter, when I was about nine years old, my father left for work in the city with the sleigh pulled by two powerful horses, which were his pride, with Gicu, my big brother. I don't know what they did, where they had been, but when they were on the road back, it was already night. Suddenly, as they passed through the Trestichii Valley, the horses began to agitate, sniffling, struggling in the harness and snapping the sled, setting off in a mad rush through the snow that came to their knees. Your grandfather, who knew what was happening, gave the reins to my brother, who was only sixteen and told him: ‚Don't be afraid, my boy! Take the horses to the village and hold them tightly, they felt a wolf but don't be afraid, I have a cure for that too!' Indeed, from the right, running through the snow, they came to them, not a wolf, but three, following the sledge. Dad had seen the wolf before, which is dangerous anyway, but when this happened to him, there was only one wolf, and they, four men armed with pitchforks and two shepherd dogs, easily put the wolf on the run. . Now, however, there were three wolves in one place, and he was only with the boy and one pitchfork, but he did not lose it. He took the pitchfork and stuck it in a bundle of corncobs, of the four he had put in his sleigh when he left, he sprinkled it with gas for the lamp, from a bottle that he always took with him and when the wolves had reached seven or eight meters behind the sled, he lit it with a match and pointed it at them. Frightened by the fire, the wolves were left a little behind, but they continued to follow the sled, giving no sign that they would give up. When the first bundle had burned three quarters grandpa threw the pitchfork, with all that fire, into another bundle, which he lit, pointing it at the wolves again. My brother held the horses well, they were sniffing and running crazily and after some time, your grandfather lit the third bundle, keeping the wolves away.

It was getting really dark and because of that snow, they didn't know how far the village was. He was worrying that he was left with only one bundle of corncobs. When he turned to stick the pitchfork in it he looked to the black sky and he saw the white columns of smoke coming out of the chimneys of the houses in Calavechi. He also lit the fourth bundle, but the wolves did not give up, getting closer and closer, so that they stopped only when the sledge entered the village and the last bundle was almost burned. As from the courtyards of the people, aroused by the smell of savage animals, more and more dogs began to bark, the wolves ran two or three times in circle and only then they headed back to the field, disappearing in the darkness. When he saw they were going away, grandpa took the reins and quieted the horses and then he yelled as loud as he could:'Wolves, maaan! Wooolves' and again like that when they turned on our street. When they entered the yard and we saw my brother white as a ghost, especially since we had heard the last cry of my father, we, the children, who had come out after our mother, we were scared and we ran into the house and she was the only one that remained outside to see what happened. Dad went down to your grandmother, untied the horses from the sleigh, quieted them and gave her the reins, saying:

„Three wolves ran after us from the Trestichii Valley to the village entrance. Take the horses with Gicu, take them to the stable! Close the door tightly and tie the horses to the stables, then take a rag, wipe them well and cover them with something. Until I come back, do not give them water to drink, as they might explode."

„I'm taking my brother and we're going to announce the people and the mayor! Those creatures might enter the village and some disaster might happen!"

„With his pitchfork in one hand and taking in the other the chain of the dog we had, he passed from our yard directly into the yard of his brother, who had also heard the cries of our father and had already left the yard. After a while, they left with two other neighbors, armed with pitchforks and three shepherd dogs, alarming people, until they reached the mayor's house. The latter, after checking his stables and pig pens, accompanied by several men with pitchforks or with bats, announced the whole village, banning the movement of people at night and ordering the closure of the inn. In our plain, there were no wolves back then as well, but sometimes, when the Great River froze, they passed from the other bank and attacked the animals of the people, but there were also people attacked and even eaten by wolves."

Listening breathlessly to his mother and trying to imagine what a wolf looks like, strangely, Codrus's face came to his mind. Five days had passed full of fear and all sorts of precautions, without him appearing at school or near it, but now he was terrified that the next day he would have to go to school and meet him again. He thought of telling his father, or Professor Elian, but neither his father nor the teacher could stay with him all the time, especially on the road between school and home.

„What happened to you, my boy? Why are you so thoughtful?"

Slightly shaking, Elaur took another donut to have time to think and said smiling:

„I was thinking about Grandpa! I didn't even know him..."

As his mother's story ended for that day when she got dressed to go out to feed the pigs and milk the goat, Elaur went to the bedroom, thinking of the captivating reading that awaited him that evening. Robinson Crusoe and his incredible story had taken over his last evenings and most of Saturday night as he fell asleep in the morning, when Martia, waking up by chance, came and turned off the light. Every time he saw that book, with glossy covers, his thoughts were running to the girl who had recommended it to him, trying to understand what she was doing at the library and how she knew that the shelf for the fifth grade did not attract him at all.

The next day, waking up at nine o'clock, after doing his math homework and eating something in the kitchen, he prepared his bag and left for school half an hour earlier.

He was determined to follow the same route. After entering the parallel street, Basamac appeared suddenly, a few meters in front of him, as he came out of a yard.

He stopped in fright, looking back first and then in front, where two elderly women were approaching, when he said in a calm voice:

„Wait for me, lad, I'm not doing you anything! Come on, I'm going to school too! I even want to ask you something! Hey, isn't your sister's name Alena?"

Hearing of Alena and aware that he had nowhere to escape, Elaur took a few steps towards him, pulling out a strangled „yes".

„Well, we've been classmates for four years!"

Having no idea about Codrus punching Elaur, he continued:

„Tell me, lad, why did you annoy Codrus so terribly? I have never seen him so upset."

Elaur knew that the incident at school, but especially the fact that he had been expelled by Professor Elian, had set Codrus off, but he said:

„Well, I don't know! I have never talked to him! I don't even know why he's mad at me!"

„Dude, you're in luck for now! You escaped him for a while. On Wednesday he was hospitalized and the next day he was sent to a hospital in the Capital. Don't get in his way, because I don't think he's going to forget too soon!"

They walked together to the school street, where just around the corner, as long as they were not seen from school, three boys in the eighth grade were smoking a cigarette.

„What happened, Basamac, boy?" Did you find relatives on this street too?"

„Yes, my boy! He's my grandpa's cousin, he said on a taunting tone. Cut the crap and give me a cigarette, because I haven't smoked since last night!"

Without looking at them, Elaur kept going, happy that at least for a while he had gotten rid of Codrus and, even more, he knew that Basamac would not bother him.

The days were much more serene for Elaur and for the others, perhaps because Basamac had also decided to pass the eighth grade, after his brother, four years older than him, said to him one evening:

„You loser! You're repeating the eighth grade because you're stupid! You were not able to pass your flunked exam! That one would have passed you even if you didn't know anything, because he also quarrels with them at the inspectorate, if they have too many pupils that flunk the exams! Stay the heck away from Codrus and Butulan and finish the eighth grade, so you can go to the tractor drivers school. Or else you will become a carrier!"

In Codrus's absence, Basamac had calmed Butulan as well, he had even helped Elaur once, when a big guy had taken their ball, with which they were playing football in the schoolyard.

Elaur had also begun to enjoy math classes, especially since he had solved the problem of his first term grades fairly quickly. He benefited from the teacher's method of proposing to solve a problem in the textbook, giving an A in the school register to the one who found the solution first.

On the other hand, in the literature class, besides the school curriculum, Mrs. Dida also explained the technique of versification with examples of joined, crossed and embraced rhymes, as well as the metric, using her fingers to count the syllables.

Captivated by what he learned, after two days, at the next literature class, Elaur came with four poems of four or five stanzas each written on his notebook. Mrs. Dida, after reading them, looked at him excitedly but also a little puzzled:

„Did you compose them yourself? Or did someone help you?"

„No, Madam head teacher! I wrote them! I really like it!"

Mrs. Dida asked him to copy them from his notebook on some sheets of paper brought from the teachers' room, which he took with her, saying:

„Keep the poems and if you compose others, bring them to me and let me read them!"

After about two days, Professor Leacu, to whom the sheets of his poems had reached, called him again to the teachers' room and after taking him out into the hall, said to him:

„Look how's the situation, boy! I like the poems you brought, but I don't want to embarass myself in the City. Make it clear for me! If you copied them from somewhere, even if only partially, nobody does anything to you, but tell me and we'll drop it!"

„I didn't copy anything, sir, and I even wrote two more yesterday but I have them at home."

„Alright. Come with me."

They both went to the library where Miss Alicia, although she had her glasses on her nose, was reading a book, holding it quite far away, with her left hand almost outstretched, while she was writing something in a notebook with her right hand.

„I came with Elaur, because I want him to write me a poem. Can he sit there at that table in the back?"

After Miss Alicia made room for him on a table in a corner by one of the three windows, Professor Leacu said to him:

„Look, I'll give you the title! I want you to write me a poem called ‚My Country'! When you finish it, you come and bring it to the teachers' room!"

Temperamental and energetic by nature, even bold with some teachers, Elaur felt intimidated in front of Professor Leacu, maybe because he was authoritarian with everyone, smiling rarely and always sarcastically. But as he liked such challenges, he was already beginning to compose in his mind the first two rhymed verses counting on his fingers the syllables of each of them.

After writing them in pencil, he continued with two more verses with a paired rhyme and the same number of syllables after which he read the whole stanza three or four times, dissatisfied with the last word. In order to replace it, he began to search and think of all the words he knew that rhymed but finding none that he liked, another pair of rhymes came to his mind. He cut the last two verses and replaced them with other two, with the respective rhymes. Now he liked the way it sounded, but it didn't work out, the last verse having one syllable less. He replaced one of the words inside the verse with one that was longer with one syllable and after reciting the stanza several times he moved on to the next stanza.

After more than half an hour, when he finished the fifth and the last stanza, looking up at the other end of the library, he saw the mysterious girl who had recommended him the Robinson Crusoe book. She was looking carefully at him, smiling enigmatically, showing him a book with brown covers, the author of which could not be read from a distance, but the title „Short Stories", written in gold like the author, but in larger letters, was as clear as it could have been. And this time she was dressed differently, wearing a burgundy velvet dress with gold embroidery around her neck, on the wide cuffs of her sleeves and on the lap covering her knees. He was dazed looking at her, with that dress and her long, wavy hair, seeming rather detached from a book on the shelves. After placing the book on the window sill, he smiled discreetly at her once more and waving goodbye to her, he disappeared into the gap between the shelves that was leading to the door.

After more than a minute, in which he looked rather confused behind her, placing the three sheets in front of him, of which only the first was written, he first went to get the book, The Short Stories by Maxim Gorky then, arriving at the librarian's office, he thanked her for the pencil and the eraser, put them on the desk, left the book next to them and asked her:

„Miss Alicia, could you please register this book for me because... I finished Robinson Crusoe and I'm bringing it on Monday because... I forgot to put it in the bag!"

„Because... because...! Learn to express yourself more beautifully without repeating the words, if you keep reading so much!"

„I got a little confused because I am nervous!"

Elaur waited confidently, feeling good when the librarian began searching for his file, telling him:

„You're in the fifth grade, right? Maxim Gorky is a bit much for the eighth grade, let alone for you!"

„Please, I am asking you from the bottom of my heart! I really want to read it! A friend recommended it to me, he lied, to be more convincing."

Holding the rather thick book in his left hand, he said to her, smiling:

„Let me see those sheets of paper too! Have you written the poem for Professor Leacu? I want to read it too! If I like it, I'll put your book in the file, if not, I won't put it!"

He handed her the sheet with the five stanzas and watched her read the poem once more and then again:

„Is that what you wrote here?"

After Elaur nodded, she continued:

„Well done, boy, I didn't know you were such a good writer!"

With the book in one hand and the three sheets in the other, Elaur waited in front of the teachers' room for about five minutes, until Professor Leacu appeared, with a school register under his arm. He handed him the sheets, holding the book close to his body without letting the cover to be visible. The teacher, changing his glasses from his nose with the ones he was using for reading, read through the poem again and again so that in the end he would reveal a big smile:

„That's it, you convinced me! I was afraid you came with poems written by others. I saw that you are talented, but prose is prose and poetry is poetry! Don't get mad at me, but I had a problem five years ago with a girl who always came to me with poems, she knew them perfectly and said they were composed by her. But something was wrog and after a while I saw one of them in a collection of poems written by high school students from all over the country. I talked to her, but she still didn't want to admit it. I searched for the brochure and after showing her the poem she burst into tears and admitted that the others were not hers either.

Chapter 5

Miraveda was a small childhood paradise, this being the easiest to notice right where Martia and Tramian had built their house, it was an extension towards the City of the village declared a neighborhood, that had only new houses and young families, with three or four children each. They didn't have much money and the houses were quite modest but the children were happy and delighted by the multitude of playmates, the charm of the games and the atmosphere of competition imposed by them, the streets resounding with their voices and giggles. Nothing seemed to disturb this small universe of joy and great hopes, the future looming in their minds as a great promise of happy times and unseen accomplishments.

As is often the case, their parents did not share the same optimism, as men's salaries were very low and women's jobs completely non-existent. For some of them, the state-owned enterprises they worked for had other advantages, especially those in the tiny food industry where they secretly scrounged various products, first for the consumption of the family. Seeing that nothing happens they took other products as well, which they traded with the neighbors, as the New Authority was still preaching that all the goods belong to the whole people. Tramian, very religious and totally devoid of such talent, had moved for some time for another job at the clothing factory in the City, where he did not even think of stealing any good that belonged to the whole people!

From the beginning of their marriage, Martia took the initiative, finding all kinds of small profitable activities and having something to do or sell all year round.

In the spring she was making money selling vegetables from her own garden where, with the exception of the frail Minela, everyone had something to do. Elaur was helping his father to dig the ground and sow and Martia and Alena took care of weeding and harvesting. Before tying strongly five or six radishes, onions or green garlic, they would thoroughly wash the ground off them. Then, the threads were cleaned of the unsightly peel and after tying the radishes were cut with scissors, the goods being ready to be exposed in order to atract the pretentious ladies from the City. In the summer, she would work on gluing the walls of the houses of various clients, with yellow clay with husk, having the reputation of being the most skilled in this profession, leaving straight walls and edges, earning well, at the cost of being exhausted by this work. In late autumn and winter, when the other activities ceased, if she was not installing the loom, with which she wove blankets and rugs for the house, she had to sew carpets with a needle, to put them on the wall or even on the bed.

From the tangled colored hanks which could no longer be used in knitting machines, bought as waste by Tramian from the factory where he worked, she would make threads of the right length, which she inserted into a larger sewing needle, fitted the two ends of the thread next to each other, joining them with a small knot and, according to a certain pattern, sewed flower outlines or various other stylized patterns on a large cloth, made of small Xs, sewn next to each other.

Once the contours were made, the work was simpler, moving on to filling them with Xs sewn with the same color or other complementary colors. After a while, when she sewed more in the afternoon and in the evening, when she was no longer working in the house, after making the model, she sewed the rest of the carpet with a certain color, it was the background, as she called it, which highlighted the previously realised pattern and the carpet was ready.

The work of sewing carpets was difficult and painstaking, especially until the contour was sewn, and no one could make such carpets, which in some cases were more than two meters long and one meter-twenty wide. That's why she had started sewing some to sale them and even if the price wasn't enough for her work, Martia was happy to bring some more money into the house to supplement the rather small budget from the cold season. She often sold the carpets that had only the contour plus the necessary strings and the client finished the work herself. Sometimes, in order to finish faster, she would give her sister-in-law, or even Alena, the routine work, that is filling the contours made by her and the background of the carpet.

„My boy, this is not a man's job", she told Elaur, taking the carpet from his hand, when she found him sewing in Alena's place, who had promised him a chocolate if she would help her.

„You have to keep studying. If you study well, I will work hard and I will keep you in school, so you can have a good job, not to struggle like your father and me."

„But I'm on vacation, Mom! I really want to help you, too, because I've seen how hard you work."

Martia looked at him lovingly, stroked his cheek, but putting the carpet aside firmly, she said:

„Mom, I'm glad you care about me but you have to keep studying! You'll be much better if you study. Look at your father! With the intelligence he has, he could've been far! But what was he supposed to do? He would go to school in the winter, with his torn shoes, full of snow and the teacher would send him back home so he wouldn't get sick. Then in autumn and spring he would be more at work on the land than at school, as I was, but at least I was a girl and I didn't need much school, at least that's what I was thinking back then."

There were a few days until Christmas and Elaur began to think about whom he would choose to go caroling with.

They were supposed to sing the carol with the star and he could choose because he was the owner of the star. It was made by his maternal grandfather, decades earlier. Martia's three brothers had also been caroling with it, in their time,

as well as his broher Nion. Made from the cylindrical wooden body of a larger sieve which formed the body of the star, it supported six thin cylindrical bars, fixed inside and wrapped in glossy yellow paper. They imitated the rays, united all around with two rows of strings that were also covered in tinsel made from the same paper.

The two round faces, made of cardboard and covered with paper of the same color, were adorned with colorful images, as they were no longer found on the market that was owned exclusively by the state, because the New Authority had wiped any religious texts or photographs. On one side was the image of the Holly Virgin with the baby, in the background of the city of Bhetlehem and on the other side, which was returned in the middle of the carol, were the three wise men, following the star which announced the birth of the Messiah.

He had to choose between Dode, the youngest of the three Urola brothers who lived opposite him and Lefan, with whom he shared fence. Both of them were his friends and classmates. He chose Lefan in the end because they were desk mates but also because the previous year, being angry with him, he had gone with Dode. December with its holidays was the most beautiful month of the year, but also the period when, with the star and the plow carols, they earned more pocket money than they received throughout the rest of the year. Choosing Lefan proved to be an inspired decision. After caroling all the neighbors and relatives of Miraveda, he insisted on going to the City center to an uncle of his, who gave them a banknote, about half of the money they had raised so far from dozens of families.

As they were happy for such an unexpected gain, they passed right by the Pescaruş restaurant, the newest and largest in the City, when they were stopped by a nice little old man who roamed the restaurants, the train station and the bus station, but also other crowded places in the City, with his eternal cigarette stub, long-extinguished and stuck to his lower lip, holding in his hand a ring of wire, on which he strung scratch tickets with which he enticed those who wished to try their luck.

Impressed by their star, as he had not seen for years, he asked them if they knew the carol well, as he didn't want to be embarassed by them and after receiving the confirmation, he entered the restaurant with them. Christmas was on a Thursday and according to the rules of the New

Authority, it was a working day, but under various pretexts the bigwigs of the city plus the regulars of the restaurant almost filled its large hall. The old man knew almost everyone in there, urging the children to sing the carol at every table in the restaurant, completely forgetting the scratch tickets he had come to tempt the partygoers with.

Once again it turned out to be their lucky day. Many large banknotes landed on a plate as big as a lid, held by the old scratch tickets seller. The banknotes were placed open heartedly by some and by others to get rid of the old man's grumbling and the laughter of others. After the restaurant tour, including singing the carol for the restaurant manager, a dizzying amount had been collected on the miraculous plate for the two children from Miraveda. At the end, the old man, who had just proved that Santa Claus existed, placed the money in a proper way and, in front of everyone, stuffed it well in Elaur's pocket, telling them:

„Now go straight home and be careful as some punks might steal the money."

Astonished and happy about the unexpected miracle of Christmas, with the eyes shining with joy, they went with great care to Elaur's house, and in the courtyard, as Lefan had asked, without unwanted witnesses, they divided all the money in two, each taking an incredible sum.

„Elaur, I want you to promise me something! Don't tell anyone how much money we've raised! Say it! You promise? I don't want my mother to know about them, because I want to buy a bicycle. I can find a used one and in the summer we will go fishing together on the Grand Canal."

Elaur could not hide the money from his mother, but to please Lefan, he put a part aside and said to his mother:

„Mom, see how lucky we are! After we went caroling to Lefan's uncle, an old man with scratch tickets took us to Pescăruș, where we toured the whole restaurant and raised a lot of money. I kept a part to get a flashlight and some books but this is yours!"

Martia, quite surprised by the amount the boy put on the table, said to him:

„What do you mean, it's mine? You're lucky! We'd better go together to the City and your mother will teach you what to buy!"

„I told you what I am going to buy. Besides, I want you to get a suit, too, like Dode's mother!"

Martia, with tears in her eyes, said to him:

„Alright, my baby! If you want, I'll buy something too, but the money is yours and you need plenty of stuff. We'll go to the City tomorrow and we'll see about that!"

Looking at him, she remembered Nion and burst into tears. Impressed, but also confused by the turn of events, Elaur asked her:

„Now, why are you crying? I wanted to make you happy and you start crying!"

As she stopped crying, Martia wiped her tears with the corner of her handkerchief and looked him in the eye:

„Why am I crying? I remembered Nion. When he died, he was just your age. God took a boy from me, but he left me an equally good one."

As he was impressed too, he remembered the promise he had made to Lefan and said:

„Mom, please don't tell anyone how much money I've raised! Lefan doesn't want his mother to know about it. If his real mother lived, maybe he would've thought otherwise!"

Martia looked at him thoughtfully and, putting her hand on his cheek, said to him, almost in a whisper:

„My boy, take care of your good soul all your life! Many will want to destroy it, to stop you from having what they never had!"

„This soul does me more harm than good. When I want to be good, like you, most people think I'm stupid!"

„Forget about them, my boy! Step aside and go on your way! After all, in life everyone goes as far as they can."

Always attentive to the meaning of what his mother said, who in a few words knew how to give him the best advice, he thought to himself, so as not to upset her: „Hey, mommy! How nice it would be to always be able to step aside!"

On the third day of Christmas, the feast of St. Stephen, Martia and Elaur took a bus from the Mill station and got of the bus after three stops, at the Palace, and from there, in five minutes, they arrived at the Two Rabbits store. The saleswoman, as she saw her, brought from the warehouse the black coat in plaid, which she had shown her at the beginning of September, at the Fair.

„Look how lucky you are! I only have this one left! I put it on sale and now it's 20 percent cheaper. Didn't you come for it?"

Martia didn't hope to find that coat anymore, but she had saved some money anyway, also for a coat. She hadn't been there earlier, because she still didn't have enough money, but now she thought that if she added the money Elaur had earned, she might as well buy him a coat. Surprised by the discount, which normally was at the end of February, she calculated that she no longer needed the boy's money. She paid it and gave it to Elaur, saying:

„I'll buy this for you, because it was my duty. We'll see what we can buy with your money but now I'm not worried anymore!"

As the coat was pretty expensive, Elaur looked at her thoughtfully for a few moments then, begging his mother to bend down a little, he whispered in her ear:

„Is my money enough to buy that suit for you?"

Martia smiled at him and, turning, winked at the saleswoman:

„What do you think of him? He also made money singing carols and decided to buy me a suit, as he saw at a neighbor. Show me that gray blouse!"

In Elaur's opinion the blouse seemed small for his mother, but she handed it to him:

„Try it! I think it's just fine!"

The boy looked at her confused at first, but then, shaking his head because his mother had taken the blouse for him, he took off his new coat, which he was wearing, as well as the old brown wool sweater, hand woven, and over the white shirt he tried the cotton and polyester jersey, buttoning up. He liked it very much and looking in the mirror mounted on a square pillar in the middle of the store, he finally enjoyed his mother's choice.

She also ordered two white shirts and some mercerized socks, also for him and when she payed, she didn't forget to add a small banknote for the saleswoman over the required amount. Then she bought him a pair of artificial leather boots and a pair of shiny black, rubber boots, perfect for the snow and mud in Miraveda. With the money left, they went to the large bookstore nearby, on the only pedestrian street in the City, unofficially called the Center, on which the young people went for a walk at the weekend.

Martia stopped by the cash register, leaving Elaur to look for what he wanted on the shelves that were full of books. He didn't have time to browse through the first book he had picked up, a hardback edition, glossy and beautifully colored, when he felt someone was looking at him insistently. He looked up and winced imperceptibly, seeing a few steps away the mysterious girl he had only met at the school library. She went to him and held out a white marble-looking hand, introducing herself:

„My name is Lexia! What a surprise to meet you! Do you want to buy a certain book, or are you just looking?"

Elaur shook slightly her rather cold hand. He was intimidated by her special clothing and by her style that was so straightforward. He forgot to say his name and he answered the question directly:

„I have some money and I want to buy some books. Not something in particular but I don't want to buy anything either!"

Taking his hand and pointing to another shelf, she said:

„Come with me, let's see what we can do! There are many good and quite cheap books, if you know how to look for them. Look, from here you can choose as many books as you want!"

She looked at him sympathetically for a few moments, smiled as enigmatically as usual and walked out, as if floating, in her sky-colored coat, with her blond hair, in long, slightly wavy strands over the hood that was the same color as the coat, edged with white fur. After watching her until she went out into the street, recovering as if from a dream, he turned to the shelf of small-format books with fairly simple covers and began to study them.

After about half an hour, counting the money in his pocket and thinking that he could buy a flashlight from the money he had earned caroling, he decided on nine books, giving up the other five or six quite hard. Anyway, he was quite happy and curious to see his mother's face when she saw him with the pile of books. He went straight to the cash register and as Martia was looking at him proudly, he paid for the books, putting them in a large black bag, sewn by Alena, at her new sewing machine, which her parents had bought in installments.

On the way to the bus station, Martia winked at him, saying:

„I don't think you have any money left for gingerbread! Come on, I have some more!"

After buying two pieces of gingerbread, made in a large black tray, right in that tin kiosk, across the bus station, they hurried across the street, because the Miraveda bus, which would pass quite rarely, was already approaching the station.

In the rumbling bus, which left immediately, they found two empty seats next to each other. Delighted by the purchases he had made, Elaur was already thinking that after four days, on the last day of the year, he would go caroling with the plow song (Plugusorul), also with Lefan, who had the best whip on their street, with gossamer, not hemp, like his.

„Mom, you don't want to eat your gingerbread?"

„This is for Minela! I don't need gingerbread, my boy!"

Elaur looked at her puzzled, then tried to break half of his triangular piece, keeping for him the part he had bitten twice, handing the other to his mother. Martia knew she couldn't refuse him and said:

„Hold it!"

She tore a small piece, leaving the rest in Elaur's hands.

„That's enough for me! You know that if you eat, I'm filled too!

After the new year he went to the City again and he finally bought a flashlight and a large, square battery for it.

„I will buy something for my mother because the money might vanish!"

Advised by Alena, who accompanied him, they went to a store called Gifts and bought his mother a beautiful scarf, a pair of socks, and a pair of cotton gloves. From the same store he bought a pair of thick gloves for his father and Alena chose a pink blouse. For Minela, they went to the bookstore, buying her a beautifully colored book and a card game called Păcălici (The Trickster). At Alena's suggestion, he also bought a game, in a flat box, on which was written with large letters, „Don't be upset, brother." With little money left, they entered the grocery shop at the stop sign, where they bought some cheap chocolates, five oranges for the five members of the family and a few hundred grams of wafers.

They walked back to Miraveda, delighted by the large snowflakes that had begun to fall, whitening everything around as if ennobling the sidewalk covered with a thin layer of frozen mud. Alena enjoyed the appearance, not at all accidental, of Nic, a year younger than her, Lefan's stepbrother, who accompanied them home. Elaur, satisfied with the gifts he bought, pretended not to notice the flirtation of the two, although he was delighted with their joy of being together, marveling at the crazy dance of the snowflakes, which seemed at least as happy as them.

Chapter 6

The winter and spring holidays were too short and the joy was ruined by the unbearable homework which did not allow Elaur to detach himself too much from the position of an obedient pupil. During the summer holidays, however, he felt much more free and like most of the boys in Miraveda he was preoccupied by all kinds of follies, which he did not even dare to think about during school, from smoking to gambling, so that on the first day of school he would abandon them completely, becoming a "good boy" and an obedient pupil again.

He had finished second the fifth grade, like the fourth grade, but he had praised at the end-of-year festivity for the first place at the City Literature Competition, his work, together with that of the girl with whom he had shared the first place, had been selected to be sent to the national phase.

At the beginning of the great vacation he had two more books to read from those bought in the winter, two more received for the second prize at school, plus two of the three won at the literature contest. During the great vacation, reading was in competition with football matches, fishing on the Grand Canal, but also with all kinds of games with the boys on his street.

He had been educated in faith in God, but he had already noticed that He was much more severe and more careful with

Tramian than with his mother. He went to work to the church in Miraveda on every Sunday or holiday with a red cross in the calendar, with the only and rare exception when he was on duty and could not change shifts with a colleague. From a very young age, Tramian went to church with his mother and from the age of seven or eight he was never absent from services, being highly appreciated by priests and loved by the whole community of believers, singing in the pew and even helping the psalm reader with his work.

On Sunday afternoons, when he was at home, he would read from the Bible or other holy books that he kept with great care. Half serious, half joking Martia sometimes said to him:

„With your faith and your prayers, husband, you drag me to heaven too! God knows I work in faith for the family and for the children."

As he was thin and peaky, Tramian had something of the appearance of the saints painted on the walls of the church, less their age and the long beard, as well as something of their piety and ascetic spirit, being content with simple and little food. Almost unnoticed by the others, he fasted on all Wednesdays and Fridays, as well as in all the fasts throughout the year, being convinced that life on earth is only the preparation for eternal life.

Martia was also a believer, but she considered that God loves you more if you are humble in your soul and if you love and respect people, being merciful to those less fortunate. Unlike Tramian who represented rather the oriental, introverted and ascetic spirit, Martia was the embodiment of the Latin spirit, her sincere faith in God and the afterlife intertwining harmoniously with the joy of living and the desire to give her children a life as good as possible.

Very enterprising, she „made money", as she liked to say, without cheating or lying, helped by her warm and kind soul. Ready to help everyone in need, she „had some sort of grudge" against those who stole, lied, or were easy but on Sundays they went to church and rolled their eyes. She relied heavily on her simple but so sound logic and also on popular wisdom, as if assuming the responsibility to pass on all the proverbs and sayings she knew. She understood well these words from the elders, using them at the right time, challenging the others to heed their teachings.

„'God gives you a job to do!' Oh... how much I despise those who complain that they are poor, but when there's work to be done they run away like partridges! God has given us hands to work and mind to think! What is good, what is not good and what we must do to be good!"

Elaur could not be as serene as Lefan, when they did the monkey business together, but little by little, he took for granted the rule that „if the parents do not know, there is no way to upset them." That's how he got to taste the temptation of gambling, with the small and ephemeral gains, but also with quite unpleasant money loss. However, he avoided dice or card games, preferring those based on skill, in which the stakes were lower and the pace of losses or gains was much slower.

He learned quickly their simple rules, but he didn't have the skills of the boys that were older than him, so in the beginning he lost the little money he had. The most popular of them, the „moon" and especially the „pit", were played with coins of the same value, thrown from a line about three meters away, to a moon scratched on the ground, consisting of concentric semicircles or a very small pit that was three to four centimeters in diameter. In the first of these, the player who threw the coin closest to the center of the semicircles won the coins of the others, and in the second, the winnings were brought by the ability to throw the coins as close as possible, or even directly into the small hole in the ground, the ones that fell around it, being then propelled into it, pushing with the nail of the thumb that had been propped on the ground. After a while, when he became some kind of champion, he earned more and more money at the pit, attracting the attention of the older boys.

„Come on, Elaur! Now you have enough money to play with us!"

Unlike coin games, tolerated by their parents, dice games, banned and hunted by the authorities, were organized in places that were hidden from their eyes. There were many stories in Miraveda about people who had gambling issues, who had lost huge sums, some of them even the houses where they lived. Elaur dodged quickly, especially since he had witnessed a few dice games, played at one of his older neighbors, in the absence of his parents, where he had seen other people he did not know and who inspired fear.

„I don't want to play dice games, because they are played by older boys, whom I don't know!"

„That's crap! You'd better admit you're afraid of your mother, said Elu, his neighbor, who had just finished his first year of high school."

Elaur let it go, especially since Elu was not far from the truth, knowing Martia's fierce character, when something seriously upset her. He made a discreet sign to Lefan, both of them going to the only grocery store in Miraveda, a rather village store, which everyone called „Collective" („La Cooperativa"). Arranged in a part of a nationalized house at the road, it had high wooden shelves on three of the walls and wooden storefronts, painted green like the shelves, with slightly sloping windows at the front, placed all around in front of the shelves to block access behind them. The only place to reach between the storefronts and the shelves was a door, no more than a meter high, fastened with two large hinges and provided with a latch on the inside, on which was put the folding counter, half a meter wide, fastened with two hinges to the window on the right and secured below, with another smaller latch.

They both sat in line with more women and children sent with „exact change" for a kilo of oil or a kilo of sugar, plus two or three of the drunks of the village, who were waiting with bloodshot eyes and trembling hands to buy their daily drug, a cheap, foul-smelling half-liter bottle of schnapps. With many products in bulk, from sugar, rice, flour and salt, to jam, halva, Turkish delight and biscuits that had to be weighed, the sale was difficult and the wait in line, which often exceeded an hour or even two, seemed a real ordeal to Elaur.

The children's torment was all the greater, as they had to stay for a long time, salivating in front of so many sweets, from which only the window of the storefront separated them and for which they almost never had money. Bulk wafers and spirals, biscuits, three or four types of chocolates, milk candies and fruit-flavored candies, some yellow, some orange or red, were beautifully placed in the shop windows, right in front of those waiting in line.

This time, with the money earned at the pit game in his pocket, Elaur was feeling something different, calculating in his mind what to buy and how much it would cost, looking at Lefan, whom he considered his guest, especially since he had lost all his money at the game.

After half an hour of waiting, when there were only two people in front of them, Lefan whispered:

„Please lend me some money, until tomorrow, when my uncle comes to us!"

As the requested amount was not big, knowing the generosity of his mother's brother, especially after her death, three years earlier, he put two coins in his palm, without asking him what he had to do with the money. Arriving in front of the counter, Elaur bought half a kilo of wafers and four spirals, which the manager put in the same brown paper bag, some biscuits and four small chocolates, as well as two hundred grams of milk candies and fruit candies. He paid the amount calculated by the seller, the same one he had calculated in his mind, and warning Lefan to follow him, he was triumphantly heading for the exit when he heard him:

„Daddy sent me to give him a pack of National cigarettes!"

Elaur, who knew that Lefan's father did not smoke, widened his eyes, but continued on his way to the door, guessing who the cigarettes were for. Arriving outside the store, after a few steps, monkeying the seemingly innocent voice of his friend, who was walking proudly with the pack of cigarettes in his pocket, Elaur said:

„'Daddy sent me to give him a pack of cigarettes!' Dude, you're such a punk!"

Bursting into laughter, he continues:

„I'm ashamed with such a deskmate!"

„Shame on you! You walk around with all kinds of candy and tomorrow when we go fishing we could watch others smoking!"

After eating the biscuits and some wafers and enjoying a chocolate at Lefan's suggestion, they crossed their street, heading for the plot on the parallel street. There they had a place to lie in the sun, but also enough pits, from where people took clay for construction and where they could hide from prying eyes. When they arrived at the place they were looking for, an older pit about two meters deep, on the edges of which had grown a lot of stinky chestnuts, providing shade, but also a very good hiding place, Lefan said to him:

„Make a bed of chestnut leaves down in the pit, because I'm going to get a match!"

He didn't even have time to finish the bed of leaves, because Lefan returned, accompanied by Damian, a friend of theirs, who lived right in the first house next to the square, but also by a boy five or six years older than them, with long hair and a mustache, very cleanly dressed and with new sneakers on his feet. Usually intimidated by strangers, especially if they were older than him, this time Elaur felt as if he had known him for a long time. He shook his hand in a friendly manner, saying his name and finding out that the nice stranger, who smiled at him very friendly, was named Favian and he lived in the Capital.

„I'm so glad to meet you, he said. I was bored as hell and I had nowhere to go. Let's see what cigarettes you have!"

When Lefan took out the National package, looking at it with some sort of infatuation, Favian said to him:

„Kind of nasty and way too strong! Look, I have a few more filter cigarettes! Who wants?"

Lefan, usually proud and stubborn, unwrapped the National package, tactfully pulled out a cigarette, prepared it a little with his fingertips, as he had seen at real smokers, took the match from Damian's hand and lit it taking a drag. Elaur, looking at Favian, who was left with the package in his hand, more so as not to ignore him, took a filter cigarette, smelled it a little to feel its special scent and lit it, puffing tactfully, as if he had been doing it his entire life. He had taken a drag in the past, at the insistence of an older neighbor, but now was the first time he had lit a cigarette just for himself and looked at Lefan, but also at Damian, who had also lit a filter cigarette from the cardboard package handed by Favian, trying not to look as a beginner in front of them. After he lit a cigarette, looking at Elaur and Damian, he asked:

„Isn't it nice? These are English! I buy them from the student campus, from foreigners. They're a little expensive, but it's worth all the money. I will go home on Saturday and on Monday I'll be back. If you want, I'll buy you a package."

Noticing the boys were quite confused and thinking that they might not trust him, he said to them:

„If you want, tell me and I'll buy for you! You can pay when I bring them!"

As the boys said neither yes or no, in order to break the awkward silence, he continued:

„I saw yesterday, when I came from the train station, that you were playing the pit game! I could teach you poker. It's a gentlemen's game and, in addition to the fun, it teaches you some psychology! It will be good for you! It's the only game in which luck, if you're a smart boy, can be fooled, if left too long to wait."

„Isn't it a card game? asked Lefan, who had told Elaur something about poker, which he had seen in a cowboy movie with his brother, Nic, at the Victoria Cinema in the City."

„Yes! It's a card game! I have a new deck of cards. I'll bring it if you want."

As the boys nodded, at about the same time Favian got up from the small ledge on which he was sitting and with easy steps, as an athlete, he headed to his grandmother's house, next to Damian's.

„Do you know this Favian? Is he reliable?" Lefan asked their friend Damian.

„He is lady Lina's nephew. He came to her in the past years, but like this, for one day. He never stayed overnight. I don't know what to say! He's a smart guy and he seems nice, but I don't know! We'll see!"

After a few minutes, Favian returned with a deck of playing cards and an old blanket, which he placed over the bed of leaves.

„Look, I'm not going to play so I can tell everyone what to do! The rules are not complicated! It is the best if you have four players, with cards from seven upwards, but if you have three or two players, you can use the same cards, but also fewer, meaning from nine upwards. For starters, you'll be playing for matchsticks. The one who deals the cards puts down the stake, in our case a matchstick, and then gives five cards to each of the players. Whoever has an opening, meaning has at least one pair of aces or kings, or two pairs or more, puts down the opening, which can be equal to or greater than the stake. If you don't have an opening, you say „check" and the next one may open. When the opening is made, the others can enter or not, paying for the opening or putting the cards on the table and leaving that turn. Those who remain in the game put down a maximum of three cards, aiming to achieve, with the cards they keep in their hand, plus the newly received ones, a combination as good as possible, in order to win the pot, meaning the stake plus the submitted openings, plus any requests, which can be „called", meaning without raising, or with pretensions („raise"), meaning you deposit as much as was requested up to you and ask for something extra.

If there are no additional claims, those who have paid all the claims show the cards and the one with the highest hand wins everything, that is, everything that has been deposited. Now, let's deal the cards and you will learn the hands along the way, depending on which cards you get!

After half an hour and about six turns, all three boys learned the game and decided to play for money, also under Favian's supervision. Lefan borrowed more money from Elaur and Damian ran to the house, coming back with the necessary money. They played for about three hours, luck being on their side in turn, they even learned to bluff, enjoying the good hands and also the art of not exposing a bad hand.

As night was coming, they decided to play six more turns and, regardless of the result, to continue the next day. After the six turns, Lefan won, paying Elaur all the money he had borrowed from him, leaving with some extra cash, Elaur beng also won but a smaller amount, Damian being the only loser.

They came out of that pit, slightly dizzy after the new game but also because of the cigarette smoke and the next day, Elaur and Lefan left the pit game for the ones that were younger than them and skipped fishing to come to play poker again. After eating a spiral, filled with a white, sweet-sour cream, they each took a mentholated candy to cover the smell of cigarettes, leaving to their homes.

In the first part of the night, Elaur dreamed only of royal flush and four aces, as well as huge pots which kept adding to the pile of money in front of him. A dream that was repeated obsessively, alternating with periods of semi-consciousness, when he knew that he wasn't playing the game in reality, so that in a few seconds, to re-enter the same dream, spinning almost hypnotically the cards he had received and winning each turn, at the expense of Lefan, but especially of the new acquaintance, Favian, who no longer looked as sympathetic as he had looked a few hours earlier, he had even begun to swear and gnash his teeth menacingly.

It was only in the morning that he got rid of the recurring dream, which was rather like a nightmare, when he began to dream of a kind of battlefield, on which he was with Lefan and where all sorts of bombs fell, seemingly invisible, producing real explosions of light and blasting terribly.

After a few minutes of writhing, in the wide bed from his room, he opened his eyes just as his mother, awakened by the lightning and thunders announcing the rain, had come to close the window onto the courtyard behind the summer kitchen.

„Did you wake up, my boy? Stay there, because I'll close the window and I'll pull the curtain, so you can sleep!"

After his mother left, he turned towards the wall, pulled his sheet over his head, falling asleep again, after the summer rain had begun and the thunder had gone away, sounding more and more muffled.

He woke up around nine o'clock, when a new series of thunder and lightning struck Miraveda and the roar of the returning rain put him to sleep again. He woke up after more than an hour, it was still raining and when he finally looked out the window, he saw through the wet gutters the neighbors' garden full of water, as he had never seen it before. The unnaturally large drops hit hard with the water surface, which covered almost the entire garden and from which only the onion sticks could be seen, thickened and with the white head of seeds on top, as well as a few dill bushes, tall and half-dry, from its dry efflorescence, directed like antennae towards the sky, the rain shook the first seeds.

He went out into the long hall, heading for the exit and opening the door of the house, protected by a small hall, which was open to the outside and looked at the flower-filled garden, which had flooded the sidewalk, bringing with it the dirty foam created by large and thick drops, as well as small sticks and dry leaves, taking them to the concrete socket, built at the bottom of the walls of the house, just to protect them from moisture.

Beyond the fence separating the flower garden from the vegetable garden, the water was also in control, almost reaching the half of the bushes with green aubergines, but also some red ones, ready to be harvested, but also those of potatoes, planted in two rows, as a green border around the garden.

After watching the wild show for a few minutes, reminiscing about the obsessive dream of playing poker and trying to find a specific explanation or meaning, he shuddered at the sound of a new thunder nearby and gave up the idea of going to the summer kitchen through the water that had also flooded the weed in front of it and he returned to his room. It was only here that he thought he could try his luck to find something to quench his hunger in the winter kitchen, which was accessible through a smaller door, right from his room. Indeed, Martia, seeing the flood outside, before leaving to work, had brought for him and his two sisters, who were still sleeping in their room, a large plate full of meatballs made in the evening, bread and a jug full of boiled milk. He ate a few meatballs with a loaf of bread and taking a cup of milk, he returned to the bedroom, where the book which he had not opened in the last two days was waiting for him. He did not leave the book until the afternoon pausing just to eat with his sisters a soup and meatballs with sauce, brought by Alena from the summer kitchen. After another hour of reading, during which Minela had come to his room a couple of times, to ask him to fix her favorite doll, which he had refused, after a few minutes she came in again, getting him stirred up:

„Minela, I told you to wait! If you confuse me like that, I won't fix any doll for you!"

She looked at him sullenly, not being used with her brother's rejection and in order to torment him a little, she said nothing, but did not look away from him. Raising his eyes from the book, he looked at her in amazement, noticing her white face and curly blond hair, not too different from the doll she was holding in her arms, except for her brown eyes, which were different from the doll's two blue beads. Satisfied that Elaur had at least stopped reading, she said:

„Lefan is looking for you!"

She returned immediately after that and went to their room, upset by her brother's repeated refusals. Elaur, in a T-shirt and pajama pants, went to the door, where Lefan was waiting for him, barefoot and muddy. The rain had stopped for about half an hour and the sky was clear and the water on the sidewalk had disappeared, leaving only dry leaves and sticks, as well as traces of mud.

„Come in the valley to see the lake that was formed in that big pit from which they carried clay with the trucks."

As he had spent so much time in the house, he returned to the bedroom, put on a pair of shorts and a blouse and they both left, barefoot, through the warm water lakes left here and there on the street.

Only when they reached the Mill Street, which ended exactly near the plot, did Elaur understand where so many floods of water had disappeared. A puddle one meter wide and over thirty centimeters deep formed in the middle of the road, disappearing in the pit of over a hundred square meters, at the edge of the plot, which was up to seven or eight meters deep.

He followed Lefan, who had passed by earlier, following the rather strange puddle for their area, which was nearly two meters wide, to cross the perpendicular street, where the water hadn't broken the ground that hard and then it was separated, like the branches of a tree, into five or six smaller puddles, through which the water still flowed, to the lake which was already over two meters deep, even three meters in some places, as they remembered the bottom of the pit.

Bypassing that pit, they headed to the place where they had learned poker the day before and where part of the brink soaked in so much rain had collapsed with the chestnuts, filling the pit with mud, leaves, and muddy water. After looking for a few seconds, Lefan, discreetly showing him the package of National cigarettes in his trouser pocket, gave him the signal to go somewhere further to smoke.

„Don't be upset, but I'm not in the mood today", whispered Elaur and after his friend made a sign of disgust, they both went back to the crowd that was gathered in the street, where Elaur recognized Favian's long, blond hair. He walked away from the others, walked over to them, and held out his hand ceremoniously, whispering to them:

„Wanna play poker? We go to my grandmother's house on the porch, where we have a table, chairs and we can play even after dusk, if we turn on the light!"

As soon as he saw him, Elaur decided to refuse him, instinctively feeling the slippery slope opening in front of him, thinking about his mother's reaction, in case she would find out:

„I'm sorry, but I really can't! I have to go with my father to my grandmother in Miraveda. I think he's already waiting for me! We'll talk tomorrow!

Lefan left with him. Lefan had already accepted Favian's proposal, going home just to get money for the game.

„Can you borrow me some more money? My uncle didn't show up because of the rain. I don't have enough and I really want to take those guys' money! If I win, I'll give it back to you tomorrow!"

Chapter 7

After refusing the poker game with the three boys, Elaur oscillated between two quite different feelings, rejoicing that he resisted the urge which he knew for sure was not to his parents' liking, but he also struggled with the obsessive image of the three at the table, feeling the thrill of the new game of chance.

He had felt, instinctively, that the game had captivated him too much and that scared him, but also the fear of the unknown had kept him away, as far as the nice, maybe too nice Favian was concerned. He felt that Favian's attraction to him was something unusual, as hard to define as it was hard to control, thinking that his nice behaviour might hide other thoughts and interests.

He had only postponed it until the next day and looking at Alena, who had stayed home because of the rain, he had an idea:

„At the farm, where you work, do they accept children my age?"

„I don't think they accept you where I work, but I've seen boys your age collecting the corn. It's not too easy and I think it's paid worse, they have only children in that team!"

„What do you mean by collecting the corn?"

„Well, how can I explain it to you? On the corn cob grows some kind of ‚baby corn'. You are supposod to break all that ‚baby corn' because it won't grow cobs. The corn is quite tall and it gets really hot in there, plus the pollen which flows on your head and under your clothes. They asked us to do that one day and from what I've seen, almost every corn cob has one or even two ‚babies'".

„That's it! I am decided! How hard can it be? If others can, why can't I? Wake me up tomorrow morning! I'm going to work with you!"

„We'll talk tonight! Let's see if mum agrees."

Alena's apprenticeship, established one year earlier, lasted only three weeks, the respective seamstress, who had never worked with any apprentice and had no pedagogical talent, abruptly announced Martia that they could not continue. As the few places at the Professional School of Chemistry had been filled and for the qualification courses organized by the Clothing Factory in the City she had to be sixteen years old, the entire following autumn and winter Alena worked with her mother, sewing carpets, so that only in May to do the qualification course from the Clothing Factory, in the pompously called profession of garment maker. As she had to wait until the autumn to be employed, she had decided to work every day at one of the state farms, established in the recent years in the dammed area, on the banks of the Great River.

Elaur also arrived there the next day, but from the farm he parted ways with Alena, who set off on foot, with a team of women from Miraveda, to the nearby lot cultivated with beans, while he climbed in another trailer, full of noisy teenagers, that led them to a cornfield. He descended among the first and, urged by the older boys, he went to the brigadier to register for the timekeeping. After writing the names of eight newcomers, he asked him:

„How old are you, lad? Are you at least two years old?"

„Yes! I turned twelve in May", Elaur replied stubbornly, to convince him that he was able to do it along with the others.

After looking at him thoughtfully for a few more seconds, he also wrote his name in the notebook with the tattered covers, from which he immediately began to call those who had already been noted in the previous days, noticing that one in two or three had not come.

„Well... There are too many absentees! The work is hard! It's easier to play football and dice games in the woods."

From Miraveda, apart from him, there were only two boys, the rest being from the City, from the neighborhood between the Main Street and the forest, that is, about three parallel streets, which stretched from The Trickster to the church in Volna, with larger and more attractive houses, but located in much smaller yards than the ones in Miraveda.

Those who heard their names, after answering, passed to the right of the brigadier, next to the new ones, getting their next row of corn. After the timekeeping and the distribution were over, work began, which did not seem difficult to Elaur at all, especially since next to him, the first that was called from the old ones, was a beautiful girl, whom he had noticed as he had climbed into the trailer.

Being about the same height as him, she had light brown hair, tied at the back, her white face being dotted with small freckles, which could barely be seen, giving her an extra charm. In addition to her beautiful features, her green eyes, with her eyelashes turned upwards, which made her look like a capricious princess, had attracted the attention of Elaur, who was very pleased with such a colleague.

He unwittingly thought about the poker game he had run away from, feeling the confirmation of an older conviction, that every time he ran away from something bad, he would receive something good instead. The girl next to him looked about two years older, but he liked a little older girls, that were bolder and curvy.

As much as he was determined to look insistently at the beautiful girl, conveying the message, „I like you," he was reluctant to talk to her, considering that it was normal for her to make the next step, which the girl next to him even did:

„Sorry... what's your name?"

He looked at her slightly confused, her question resembling too much the way you approach young children, when you want rather to hear them speak than to know their names. He cleared his throat to make sure he wasn't choked with emotion:

„My name is Elaur!"

„You can call me J. K.!"

„Jeca? But that's not how he called you at the timekeeping!"

„My name is Leta, but at school, a girl who doesn't like me once called me Jeca, instead of Jecu, which is my last name. In order to spite her, I chose the pseudonym J.K. and all my friends have been calling me that way ever since. With a capital J and K for kilogram!"

„Do you mind if I call you Leta? I like the way it sounds, it's a really nice name!"

„You can call me how you want! I'm glad you like my name! I like your name too. It sounds Spanish. I haven't heard the name Elaur either. I heard the name Laur, but I like the way Elaur sounds!"

As they kept talking, Elaur told her that he also knew some boys who lived in her neighborhood:

„From time to time we play football with them in the woods. We represent the team from Miraveda, they represent the team of the forest. Make, Eci, Mari and more. Tita, although he lives in Miraveda, next to me, plays in the forest team.

„Well, Make is my cousin and my friend, the girl over there, is Mari's sister!"

Pleasantly surprised, Elaur looked at the indicated girl, noticing immediately that she looked a lot like her brother, but she was shorter and much fatter than the big fella Mari, from the forest team.

„I think you know Jeny too! She also plays football!"

„How can I not know her? Those who just pass by know her, let alone me, who played football with her. She plays on the forest team and is better than many of the boys. Once, when they were attacking and I was playing in the defense, she hit me in the face with the ball and I thought the train had hit me!

„ Do you come often to the forest? We've also been down there, but we never saw you!"

„In our team play the boys that are older than me. They schedule matches, and I play less often, only when one of them is missing."

Until the lunch break the time passed quickly and unexpectedly pleasantly, Leta asked him quite direct questions, but which he liked:

„What do you like more, math or literature?"

„Literature. But for a year now, since I have another teacher, I also like math."

Their discussion, led by Leta, not only pleased him, but also made her more and more interested and curious:

„As far as I believe, you are really the top of your class!"

He was somewhat confused by her straight to the point style, so he didn't know how to react, so as not to look nerdy or arrogant:

„For me, the top of the class is the one who takes the first prize, and I took the second prize. The top of the class, in addition to having better grades than mine, has a more beautiful writing than the girls and some perfect notebooks. It annoys me too! I think he only writes and studies all day long!"

„Well, what else do you do?"

„Ooh! I have a gang on the street, as I don't think about homework at all! My French notebook is always with Mira, my cousin, who is my colleague and who, after doing her homework, writes mine as well. In general, I do my homework with pleasure when it comes to literature and mathematics, but I'm not very passionate about the rest."

At lunch, when everyone ate what they had brought from home, Leta went to eat with her friends, somewhere on the grass burnt of the sun, over which they placed a blanket, a little bigger than a towel, each unfolding their packet, with cheese or salami, but also homemade meatballs, boiled eggs and many tomatoes. Elaur, who did not know the two boys from Miraveda very well, sat alone on a small mound, eating quickly and somewhat absent-mindedly bread with sheep's cheese and two boiled eggs, right from the piece of white paper in which they had been packed by his mother.

He glanced at the group of girls, who were whispering something, giggling slightly and stealing him curious glances,so that he immediately turned his head to their friend Leta, who was telling them something in a whisper. Elaur felt targeted, even bothered to be the subject of their discussion, but after a while, noticing the admiring looks of Leta's friends, he had a feeling as unknown as it was pleasant, being almost certain that Leta liked him and she spoke well of him.

After eating, entering the cornfield, to continue the work, he was unpleasantly surprised that a big fella, at least four years older and one head taller than him, who had already given him the evil eye, had changed places with a girl, taking her row on Leta's right side. He was a neighbor of hers, who wanted to warn him when she went to the barrel with drinking water:

„Hey you, little boy! Mind your own business in Miraveda and just stop playing the smart guy with Leta! She's my girlfriend, and if you're still slick, you might end up drinking water with a straw!"

Elaur was not a coward, but looking at the big fella, who the body of a buffalo, having a lot of friends among the boys in their group, he immediately realized that he had no chance if he ignored him, much less to defy him. Without saying anything, until Leta returned, he began to quickly break the baby corn on his row, managing to reach more than twenty meters in front of her, when she shouted at him:

„Elaur! Wait for me! I'll catch up with you right away!"

Angry with her for not telling him about the big fella, but much angrier because she had a „friend", he didn't answer or stop, breaking the baby corn even harder, as if they were monstrous extensions of her unbearable neighbor. Seeing that he wouldn't stop, Leta quickly understood what had happened and left the work, she caught him up quickly, at some distance from the big fella, who was watching her grinning and taking Elaur gently by the hand, she asked:

„What did this sucker tell you? I knew that's why he moved near me!"

„He told me you were his ‚girlfriend' and to leave you alone!"

„Maybe in his dreams! He's a big loser who's been following me for about two years and doesn't understand that I'm not interested! Ignore him and that's it!"

Elaur looked at her confused, with a crooked smile, without saying anything more, and thinking about his threats. Leta quickly understood how things were and motioned for him to wait, turned on her heels and went resolutely to her neighbor. Elaur did not hear what they were saying, but before long, without much noise, he was lost among the rows of corn, and in his place appeared, smiling, the girl he had changed places with. As he got rid of the big fella's presence and impressed by Leta's power over him, Elaur began to break the baby corn on her row, in reverse, until they met:

„You feel good now, okay?" she told him, with a seductive smile.

It was the second time, in less than an hour, that Elaur had experienced that overwhelming sensation, which had conquered his mind and soul, making him happy.

„You don't have to be afraid of him! For every yin there is a yang! If he still upsets you, I'll take care of him."

More than half an hour before the tractor with the trailer came to take them back to the City, the two finished their rows of corn. They bypassed the cornfield on a dirt road to the left, heading to the other end, where they had left their belongings. Shortly after passing by those who were still working in the cornfield, Leta took him by the hand, making him simply float and completely forget about the unbearable big fella, but also about the fatigue of the first day of work in his life.

After everyone in the cornfield returned, with the knowledge specific to girls, who are much more evolved than boys in adolescence, Leta asked him to give her the hand, to get in the trailer. It was a special gesture, like an investment, that confused Elaur, but it also made her very happy, especially in front of the big fella and the boys in her neighborhood, who were thus informed of her choice.

Arriving at the farm, waving his hand, Elaur no longer climbed into the trailer with Alena, but stayed with Leta in the trailer with which they had come from the cornfield, and passing through the City, where almost all descended, continuing their way to Miraveda, where the tractor and trailer were parked overnight.

Standing, like everyone in the trailer, Leta approached his ear, saying:

„I hope you'll keep coming at work! Many come one day and then you don't see them again!"

Elaur, overwhelmed by her attention, noded, and he was immediately surprised by the light brake of the tractor driver, who projected Leta towards him. When her breasts were close to his chest, he felt an unnatural heat invade his entire body, unlike her, who behaved just as naturally, making fun of the event.

He also smiled in the end, especially since the happy event was repeated two or three more times, feeling not only her breasts pressed to his chest, but also her breath very close to his lips. It seemed to him that time had run faster than ever, until the trailer stopped where Leta and everyone in her neighborhood had to get off. She did not go down immediately, waiting for the others to come down, which assured Elaur it was also difficult for her to leave.

„Goodbye! See you at the farm tomorrow. I hope you'll have beautiful dreams tonight!" she whispered.

As the trailer headed to the Main Street, she waved at him, looking at him with a smile, and he watched her until the tractor turned left toward Miraveda.

Still smiling, euphorically, Elaur went down to the Mill and went home, where his mother received him quite surprised, seeing him so happy, when she expected him to be exhausted after his first day of work.

„What's the matter with you, my boy? Why are you so happy? I was thinking of not letting you go! What, we have nothing to eat?"

„Yes, I'm going! It's not that hard and there are a lot of kids my age. I raise money for the Fair and I will also buy books!

Martia looked at him fondly, considering that, after all, work did not hurt him, adapting him to hard work and making him love school even more. Elaur was proud, in his turn, that he worked and that he earned his money, which seemed much more valuable and real than the money earned caroling and more „honest" than what he earned at the pit game.

After another two days, the relationship with Leta, materialized especially in their innocent dialogues and looks, in a few handshakes or thrilled touches, but especially in the special feelings shared by both, seemed to turn into a beautiful story. On the fourth day of work, when the trailer in which he had climbed at the Mill arrived in Leta's neighborhood, Elaur could not distinguish Leta's face, in the compact group waiting for the trailer to stop. Slightly intrigued by her absence, he watched the people climb on the trailer, hoping that Leta was only late and would show up at the last minute. After the trailer left, he looked questioningly at her friend, who was making room among the others, for him:

„Leta felt bad last night and went to the hospital! I talked to her mother, she is having appendectomy today!"

For Elaur, Leta's friend's words fell like a hammer. He didn't know how to react, even remembering a neighbor of his, who almost died because his appendicitis had „broken," he asked, choked by emotion:

„It is something serious? What did her mother tell you?"

„She told me that she felt better in the morning! If she has surgery today, she'll be in the hospital for another four to five days."

Elaur, who had retreated thoughtfully into a corner of the trailer, stared bitterly to one side, avoiding the big fella's satisfied grin, thinking he deserved to be punched in his stupid face, no matter how hard he would beat him afterwards. Noticing his reaction that was at least strange, Leta's friend intervened irritably:

„Why are you laughing? Do you think that if she has surgery, she will like you? Get the hell out of here! Leta is right when she says there is no bigger loser than you!"

As they were not going to the farm the next day, being Sunday, Elaur kept thinking about how to get to the hospital, to Leta, even if he did not even know where the hospital was, much less in which ward to look for her. Eventually, he realized for himself that he could not go to her on the first day after the operation, and he spent his Sunday quite downcast.

Monday morning, as he met Leta's friend, his first concern was to ask her how she was feeling.

„She had surgery on Saturday, but yesterday they only received her mother for a visit, because she was still in intensive care. Her mother told me that she was fine and that if there were no complications, she would get out on Wednesday or Thursday."

Elaur also went to work on Tuesday, more to find out from Leta's friend the number of the ward where she was moved after the intensive care. In the morning, but also on the way back, he climbed with Alena in the trailer that took him directly to the farm, because the big fella, but also one of his friends, had threatened to beat him.

On Wednesday, he gave up his job at the Farm, but at five o'clock in the afternoon he was in front of the gate of the old hospital in the City, but without success, the visits being allowed only on Sunday. Without any information, at the risk of being beaten, on Saturday he waited in Leta's neighborhood for the trailer coming from the farm and followed her friend, who smiled at him as an accomplice, but gave him bad news:

„Leta got out of the hospital on Friday, but went to the country, to her grandparents. She'll be back in early September!"

He headed to Miraveda in low spirits, trying to understand why Leta had left to the country, without leaving him any message, remembering all the time he had spent with her and thinking that he had not upset her at all. The memory of the three days and her green eyes brightened his face, determining him to be optimistic and confident that they would see each other again in early September.

Chapter 8

„Elaur! What's wrong with you, my boy? I noticed you've been sad for a few days. Did something happen to you and you don't want to tell me?"

„I'm sorry I can't go to the farm anymore. If it weren't for those bastards I told you about, I would've kept going, he said, though he wasn't in the mood for the farm or the work, which in Leta's absence seemed hard and poorly paid. He couldn't tell his mother he was unhappy, especially since he hadn't told her anything about Leta and his feelings.

„Come on, my baby! Get out of the house! My brother-in-law from Calavechi came with the cart, to bring us half a sack of flour. Don't you want to go to them for a few days?"

Martia had a younger sister in Calavechi, who lived opposite the church and two brothers, each with his own family, the younger one living right in the old house where she had grown up, and who had remained his, after their mother had died two years earlier. Elaur saw with his mind's eye the two huge pear trees in his grandparents' yard and thought of the small, sweet pears that had probably ripened, but also of his cousins from Calavechi, the other brother's daughter and boy, who had their house up on the hill, on the edge of the village. Considering the impossibility of meeting Leta and hoping that with his cousins from Calavechi time will pass more easily, he accepted his mother's proposal and got out in the yard to greet his uncle. The latter, a huge man, with red cheeks and always with a smile on his face, wearing some kind of rubber apron, was giving water to his two horses harnessed to the cart, from a metal bucket, which he also supported with one knee.

„Come, my nephew, to the country! The first watermelons are ripened and if the weather keeps being that warm, in two or three days the cantaloupes will also ripen!"

Martia, with her kind soul, although born the third of the seven brothers, was, in a way, a good mother for all. For her brothers and sisters, but also for brothers-in-law, sisters-in-law and their children, even addressing her by the nickname „auntie". Knowing that he was welcome at any of his mother's siblings, Elaur put some spare clothes into a nylon bag and left with his uncle's cart to Calavechi, where they arrived just before noon.

Glad to see him, his aunt, who had just finished cooking, quickly set the table in the yard, in the pleasant shade of a large walnut tree, between the fountain and the summer kitchen. Martia's sister, who looked very much like her but had blue eyes, loved Elaur very much, especially after the accidental disappearance of his brother Nion.

„You're a big boy now, Elaur! My sister told my you're the top of the class! She's very proud of you! Let's eat, and then your uncle will cut that big watermelon over there! We know it's sweet and good, because we have already checked it, so not to fool ourselves!"

After a rather fine week, spent with his cousins in Calavechi, but in which his thoughts kept running to the beautiful and temperamental Leta, he returned to Miraveda with an old, dusty bus, whose engine stopped, even while parked, at the station in the center of Miraveda, refusing to start, despite all the repeated attempts of the driver. Unlike the passengers who went to the City, Elaur was not upset at all to get off a stop before the Mill. On the contrary, he thought he might stop by his classmate, who lived right next to the school, to retrieve a ball he had left with him on his last day of school.

Going down there, in front of the church, he returned a few steps, passing the dispensary in the building next to it, where some years earlier the Miraveda town hall had functioned and crossed that street, perpendicular to the road, to the summer garden of Strugurelul restaurant, which had the entrance from the road. Approaching the high fence of the summer garden, made of slats fixed diagonally and painted green, forming small diamonds through which one could see inside, Elaur recognized Codrus's unmistakable face at one of the tables, staring at the road, frowning as always. At first, he froze in fear, and then, realizing that he had not been noticed, he continued to walk at the same speed, so as not to attract attention, on that alley, away from the road and always looking back, until he reached his second street parallel to the road where his colleague lived.

After taking the ball, he hurried home, thinking of Codrus's return to Miraveda, which, added to Leta's departure, to her grandparents' village, about twenty kilometers down the Great River, made him feel even more sad than he was when he had gone to Calavechi. Luckily everyone in the family was gone, so he went to the summer kitchen, which was never locked, took the key of the house from the cupboard, high to the ceiling, unlocked the hallway door, and entered.

Arriving in his bedroom, he felt suddenly refreshed, looking at his beautifully arranged books on the table, waiting for him like faithful friends. He had missed them, and since his bedroom was the coolest in the house, he felt an unspeakable pleasure in immersing himself in reading. He read with pleasure, almost greedily, forgetting about everyone and everything, completely disappearing into the story and missing everything else hour after hour, as if leaving his own body, traveling to unseen lands with the characters of the book, who were taking over his mind and soul.

Two more weeks passed in which he read a lot, going out only in the yard, from time to time, to fulfill the task entrusted to him by his mother, to take care of his younger sister. As he had established himself the clear rule of not going out into the street, her two friends, of the same age as her, came daily to play together, on a mat sitting in the thick shade of the acacias behind the house.

On the first day of September, he woke up in the morning thinking of Leta, hoping that she had returned from her grandparents. After eating margarine and marmalade on bread, sipping a mouthful of green tea made by Martia before going to work, he put on a pair of long pants and a clean cotton blouse and headed to Leta's neighborhood.

After three days in a row, in which he had wandered through her neighborhood, to no avail, on the fourth day, on the Mill Street, from which she usually reached on the road, he met Leta's friend, who came to Miraveda, to some relatives:

„Leta moved with her family to the country, at her grandparents! Her father took a job on the farm there and they all moved."

Her words had fallen like a black curtain in Elaur's mind, who, bewildered, could not even ask anything more, as he was surprised and nervous but also because of the presence of a classmate of his, who lived across the street. He left dejected and discouraged, with the strange feeling that something invisible and much stronger than him had decided he wasn't going to see Leta again.

In the years that followed, he would remember her from time to time, as a beautiful dream, meeting her only seven years later, by chance, walking through the Great City Park, hand in hand with her husband. They recognized each other immediately, he looked at her nostalgically, and she smiled discreetly and a little bitterly.

The next two years had passed quite quietly, Codrus did not appear at all at their school or in Miraveda. Elaur even found out, with great joy, that he was a construction worker, in the city declared a county seat, located about forty kilometers further north, living in some barracks on the construction site.

Elaur had the same respect for school, although at home he didn't study a lot, being content himself only with his homework, opening the textbooks only when he needed them to find a solution. But he was very attentive in class, managing to remember most of the new lessons, obtaining very good marks, and in the seventh grade he even took the first prize for the first time, with only a few steps behind Arian, who was top of the class.

He was loved by teachers and even overlooked sometimes, when he was making some blunder, only for his attention during the lessons. In fact, Licea , the geography teacher, reserved five or six minutes for him, after teaching the new lesson, in which he said a summary of it, which forced him to be even more attentive.

„Come on! Major Elaur! Tell us the new lesson again, maybe something will remain in the minds of these fools, because I don't think they will open the book at home!"

Elaur's class was the best of the four in the same year, but there were also enough of his classmates who did not learn anything at home and did not study hard. Mr. Licea had nicknamed him Major, after the rank of his uncle, Martia's older brother, whom the professor had met on a trip to the mountain town where his garrison was located. As he loved geography, history and nature, father Licea, as all Miraveda knew him, organized the most beautiful excursions, presenting to the pupils directly almost everything he taught them in geography lessons, but also many other things, useful in history and biology.

On the first announced trip, fearing that something might happen to Elaur, Martia had kind of hesitated to let him and only after she had come to school and talked to Mr. Licea, evoking the loss of her first son, did she agree. After returning from the trip, seeing how many new things Elaur had learned and how excited he was, when she met the teacher, she thanked him:

„Mr. Licea, no matter how many more trips you organize from now on, put Elaur first on the list. What you do is very good for these children. You open their mind as many of them, without your trips, would not have left Miraveda."

They were cheap and beautiful trips, professor Licea choosing special routes, with accommodation and very cheap meals, in dormitories and school canteens, from cities with many historical objectives, located in extremely picturesque areas.

On such a trip, at the beginning of the sixth grade, Professor Licea had discovered Elaur's qualities as a poet. He took care, together with the music teacher, of the participation of their school in the annual competition between the schools from the City, preparing the choir of the school from Miraveda, but also the content of the entire artistic program. Subscribed, year after year, to the first prize with the choir, his opinion mattered when it came about the decisions related to the rest of the program, deciding on the spot that Elaur is the new poet of the school. In addition, when they came back in Miraveda, he decided that Elaur was to join the two girls who presented the artistic program, which in addition to the three or four choral works, also included solo musical performances, but also dances, recitations and a play.

„Major, if you could sing, I would have taken time off and went on vacation, joked Professor Licea."

Indeed, Elaur, who had won the recitation contest, but also the first place with the play, becoming a little star, was delighted by the girls' attention and the teachers' appreciation. More recently, he had been co-opted into the school's football team, where he met the boy from class B, who was said by everyone to be the smartest pupil in the school, which made him curious, but which he would be convinced of quite quickly, especially after finishing middle school, when they became classmates in high school.

Elaur had a vocation for competition, which helped him many times in his life, but which sometimes made him unbearable, both in rummy and card games, but also in football and other games, as he would become irascible when he lost. He even knew, instinctively, that he needed competition to mobilize, seeking to meet and compete with the best.

„I heard you're very good at math, he told Peter, the boy from class B, after a football game. I have an interesting geometry problem, which I found a solution to, but I want to see if it's correct."

He handed him half a sheet from a notebook with squares, which he unfolded, leaving only his drawing and the statement of the problem. He wanted not so much to test him as to approach him, feeling that he would only gain from the relationship with him. The next day, during the big break, Peter came to him in class and sat down on the bench with him and said:

„I really liked the problem. I struggled a little with it, but I think I found the right solution."

He showed him the paper he had come up with on which was the solution to the problem, quite different from the solution he had found and after confronting the two solutions, Peter sincerely acknowledged that Elaur's solution was simpler. In turn, Elaur was amazed by the graphic construction invented by Peter who, not noticing a certain parallel, had not given up, developing a solution he would never have thought of. They both enjoyed what would eventually turn into a long friendship, with Elaur appreciating Peter's tenacity and extraordinary intelligence, which gave him great mobility of thought and he, feeling provoked by the ambition of his new friend, rejoiced that he had found a friend, who was quite competitive.

Before the eighth grade, they had also started meeting during the summer holidays, looking together for solutions to complicated math problems. Peter never refused such a challenge and Elaur tried to get away, at least from time to time, from the gang on his street, from the endless football matches, after which they felt exhausted, but also from the poker games, the other „sport" that had taken over their street.

After such a bout of mathematics, returning from Peter, who lived in Miraveda, diametrically opposed to where he lived, he got hungry and stopped at the Bread Center, as they pompously called the store on the road, on the opposite side of the restaurant. Being the only place in Miraveda where people could buy their bread on the card, it had for sale pretzels, croissants and other specialties, the famous „twins" and „Japanese", which were brought with the bread and sold out in two or three hours. Although there were many people in line, once inside, the image of the fresh „Japanese", braided quite interestingly and well garnished with small poppy seeds, wouldn't let him go.

The ones in line had waited for more than two hours for the bread car, which arrived at Miraveda once a day, at a time no one knew, and was unloaded by a few older boys, among those waiting, who thus obtained the right to be served among the first. The others in the queue, a few women and many children, older or younger, were standing in three or four quite crowded rows and they were especially careful not to be preceded by anyone. He thought he had to wait quite a long time, the queue advancing rather slowly, because the vouchers, torn from their yellow cards with black numbers, required also half a loaf of bread. The manager used a long, well-sharpened knife to cut the fresh bread on the wooden grill, not being allowed, nor able, to give more bread than each had the right with the card, issued in relation to the number of people in the family.

As soon as he sat in line, a girl appeared in the doorway of the store. She had passed like him in the eighth grade, being in class C and meeting him in line, languished for him, sitting right behind him in the row next to the counter. She was wearing a red dress with small white flowers, a fashionable miniskirt, incredibly short and fitted to the body. As Elaur didn't pay much attention to her at school, being interested in other girls, this time, that dress, which highlighted her beautiful body and well-developed breasts for her age, had immediately attracted his attention. In addition, the girl's pelvis, located quite high, made her straight legs look even longer, making Elaur feel an irresistible attraction, probably accentuated by the wave of pheromones transmitted by her.

„What are you doing, dear Elaur? I haven't seen you much at our place, at the Bread Center," she whispered, approaching his ear.

„I thought the top of the class only ate cake!"

She pressed her big, firm breasts against his back, making him feel an unnatural warmth that flooded his whole body, his cheeks were burning and his pulse was galloping like a ragged horse.

„Hi, co ... colleague!, he replied, confused that he only knew her last name. I also didn't know you could be so ironic. I don't really come here! We are registered at the Small Market Bread Center in the City. Now I'm coming from a friend and I'm hungry! Look at the queue I have to stand for a ,Japanese'!"

More and more people were sitting behind them and on the side, giving the girl the opportunity to cling even more to him, without attracting anyone's attention. Elaur had never felt that carnal pleasure before, so he was overwhelmed by the situation and he would answer her simple questions quite foolishly. He didn't know how many minutes they had been in line, as time was turning into a hot, dizzying liqueur, his hormones went completely crazy, when the girl intentionally pushed her right leg between his legs, as naked as hers, because he was wearing shorts and a thin T-shirt. Some kind of manliness was growing in him, as if awakened from a long sleep and looking ahead, without seeing or hearing anything, he felt how those around him had melted, simply disappearing. After a while, he was brutally brought back to reality by the thick, slightly annoyed voice of the salesman, who was looking at him, his hand outstretched to his banknote:

„Come on, lad! Should I wait longer for you to tell me what you want?"

„Please give me a ,Japanese' one! Well..ooh ...! No! Wait a minute! Give me two ,Japanese'!"

He took the two ,Japanese', plus the change and he left the store completely dizzy, without looking at her. He was waiting outside, thinking of offering her a ,Japanese', too when, after a while, she came out with two loaves of bread in a nylon bag and ignoring him, she went to two women who were talking, addressing one of them so that he too could understand:

„Come on, Mommy! A little more and I could've spent the whole day in line!"

Then she looked at him, smiling discreetly, like an uncertain promise, leaving with her mother, in the opposite direction to where he was supposed to go, walking in a studied way, knowing she was seen and even wanted. Elaur was speechless, with his hormones pumping all over his body, staring like an oddball behind her.

He watched her until they reached the first corner, from where, crossing the road, before disappearing on the street leading to the school, avoiding her mother, she looked at him once more insistently, making a discreet sign with her hand. Only then did he go home, dizzer than after ten math problems, so that after a few hundred meters, he realized how stupid he was that he had not followed her from a distance, to find out where she lived.

Chapter 9

When he got home, after eating something on the run, he returned to the wooden bench at Elu's gate, which he had just passed and where several boys on the street had started playing a game of poker. As two of them had just run out of money, as did those on the sidelines, who were standing and chatting, he immediately entered the game, losing at first more than half of the money he had brought with him. Slowly, understanding the game of Elu, who was five years older than them, but also the bluffing games of Lefan, he began to win, helped by the incredible series of good cards, which came almost hand after hand, exasperating them all.

„The one who is lucky in the game is unlucky in love", those on the side teased him, who did not suspect how well these words were describing him, when Lefan went all in like a madman and Elu decided to fold.

Elaur remembered that Lefan had kept three cards, putting down only two, compared to him who had put down three cards, keeping a pair of queens in his hand. He started checking the cards he received, the first being also a queen. He thought that if Lefan had three aces or three kings, he would be better than him, checking the next card, which was an ace. But he was startled when he saw the last card, which was also a queen, so he had four of a kind, queens.

Being confident enough, knowing that Elaur had put down three cards, having at most one pair, compared to him who had three kings from the beginning, Lefan told him:

„Come on, man, it's getting dark until you decide!"

Elaur, who had put down a king and had an ace in his hand, was already certain that Lefan could not have four kings, nor a royal flush, as he didn't have the queen. As the only possibility for Lefan to have a better hand than his four queens was the flush, that is, five different cards of the same suit, Elaur said to him:

„Because you don't have any money, I won't raise anymore, to put you in debt. I will call, but you're gonna be the first who shows the cards!"

„Full house, kings over aces," Lefan showed the cards, sure of himself.

Elaur waited a second and slowly unfolded his cards:

„Four girls," he said, putting down the four queens and blowing them all up.

After the uproar and all the comments made by those around him, remaining in the game only with Elu, also winning, they decided to stop the game, as it was already getting dark. Elaur had earned quite a nice amount of money, to which the other boys had also contributed, who had been „relieved from the burden of money" until he came, even by Elu and his cousin, Lefan, his colleague.

„Now that you've won, maybe you disappear again for two or three weeks," said Lefan, who still didn't understand how he could lose, with the biggest full house in that game.

„Go and thank the icons for the luck you had," he teased Elaur, visibly angry.

After assuring him that he would play the next day, Elaur put the money in his pocket and went home, thinking of the novel he had started the night before, but also of what had happened with the girl at the Bread Center.

The next day he lost most of the money he earned from Lefan and especially from Nic, Dode's middle brother, and in the evening he decided to go to work at the Farm with his classmate, who lived next to the school and from whom he had learned that it was paid very well for their age. He was making again a name for himself, earning „his money", through work, especially since for three months he also had an identity card, in the previous two years taking his money from the Farm with the birth certificate. He was, in fact, trying to escape the games of poker, but also the passion for gambling that his mother had frightened him with.

Pulling the dried bean plants out of the ground, work he had done with his colleague, did not seem so difficult, especially in clean areas of grass, but he had great trouble, after only three days, with the wounds on his fingers, in the area of the nails, caused by the dried beanstalks, but especially by the long and resistant threads of the dwarf morning glory plant, which stretched two meters long and which were wound on several beanstalks, making their plucking an incredibly difficult operation.

He didn't like to give up, though after two or three days his fingers were always bleeding. He had already tried to wear gloves in his hands, but they slid along the stalks, tearing the beans from the earth that was hard as stone being cumbersome or even impossible. The only solution was to bandage all his fingers, making smile all the women in Miraveda, many of them his mother's age and who did not have this problem, as they had rough hands. Bandaged and avoiding being seen by his mother, he was stubborn to go on, eventually reaching twelve working days. After the first few days, following the example of the others, he had also put some beans in his shirt, coming home with a kilogram and a half, maybe two, of beans, he put it in the kitchen and forgot to show it to his mother, but the next evening, when he put almost two kilograms of beans in front of her, she looked at him and said, angrily:

„Well, my boy, you want them to catch you at some control and embarrass you! God forbid they made fun of you at school too! I'd better buy it! I told you, if you study hard, I have no other claim from you. And then, you don't get rich on stealing!"

Martia liked to say this, which she had known since she was little and when fortunes, small or big, were in people's hands and not in the state's hands, as they were at that moment. She respected this saying however, like Tramian, although they both saw, in Miraveda and in the City, what houses and fortunes were made by those who stole from state-owned enterprises, without anyone holding them accountable. Tramian even philosophized, during discussions about religion, for those who wanted to listen to him:

„The new Authority does much harm, as it wants to take God out of people's minds. God is the best guardian. He's guarding everything and he doesn't even ask for a salary! They put guards everywhere, but who keeps the guards from stealing?"

After the twelve days worked at the farm, in the evening at dinner, Martia noticed that Elaur kept hiding his right hand under the table and said:

„I want to see what happened to your hand! Come on, like at school, hands on the table!"

Elaur, who had counted his earnings from the farm for fifteen days, did not hesitate and showed his hand, looking rather stubbornly at his mother.

„Lord! What happened to your fingers? Those are real wounds! And you want to go to the farm again, in this situation? I'd have to be crazy to let you go!"

„I will protect them with adhesive bandage and there will be no problem! I'm going for three more days, to reach fifteen, as I agreed with my colleague!"

„No more ‚fifteen'! You're not going anymore! I didn't realize earlier that you wouldn't have reached even ten days! After we eat, I will bandage them with ointment and where they are swollen, I'll put Rivanol!"

Elaur was also worried about the way his fingers looked, he had understood that there was no need to insist and was glad that he had at least something to read. The next day he woke up at nine o'clock, more to urinate in the toilet at the back of the yard, but he returned to his bedroom and slept for another hour. After waking up a second time, he enjoyed some more time in bed, maybe for a quarter of an hour, perhaps because of the cloudy weather outside and after studying his rivanol-yellowed bandage, he untied it and put small pieces of tape back on.

The cloudy skies and the southerly winds made the air much more breathable than during the previous days.

He went out into the courtyard, and seeing his father making a net of wire, he approached him:

„Hello, daddy! How's business?"

„If I turn the crank, it works. If I stop, it stops too, Tramian joked, looking at him facetiously."

Elaur watched him for a while, as he was spinning the crank and the wire was profiled by a blade that spun in a steel cylinder, it came out like a sinusoid and, continuing to spin, entered through all the meshes formed by the previous wire.

Tramian had been working for two years in the new straw cellulose and paper factory, built just six or seven years earlier by the English, who had been in the City for almost three years, they impressed its inhabitants with their skill, but also with the heavy drinking they organized on Saturday night. Before the arrival of the English, engineers, technicians and workers, but also their families, a total of about a hundred people, the first two blocks in the city had been built for them and an English Club had been set up in the building where it had once been the City Casino.

From the factory, Tramian bought at the price of waste the wire that remained from the straw bales, cut before they entered the shredder, using it to make a net, struggling to insert a piece of wire into the machine, for each row of nets. Elaur had seen at Lefan's father, who also had a netting machine, how the wire was taken from a coil bought from the trade and only had to be cut with pliers when the turn was over. Impressed by his parents' ingenuity in finding new sources of income, he said to his father:

„It would work faster if you used wire in a coil! You're right but, you see, the wire costs me less than a quarter than the one in the coil! I sell the net cheaper than everyone else and I earn better!"

Elaur asked him if he wanted to eat bread with cheese and tomato with him, and his father said:

„Gather more tomatoes and wash them, because I'm coming too! Beware that some tomatoes are tied with a blue thread! You must not pick them up, or even touch them, so they won't break!"

While he was picking the tomatoes, in a wicker basket with a high handle, his father also came and while he was washing the tomatoes, he also washed himself with a handful of laundry detergent to remove the stains and the grease from his hands.

„What do you do with the tomatoes that are tied with a blue thread? They are the largest and the most ripe!"

„That's why I kept them! We let them ripen until they fall off by themselves and only then do I take the seed and dry it. I want to make the shelter bigger and in the spring to make seedling for us in the yard, but also for sale."

„You don't eat cheese?" Elaur asked, seeing that he ate only bread with tomatoes.

„It's Friday, my boy. I have all the time in the world to eat cheese."

Elaur swallowed his words, looking at his father's rough, frayed and cracked hands and then looked at his own, when his father, looking at his hands and showing them his, said:

„The work is hard, my boy! Look! That's why you have to study hard! It's a good thing that you went to the farm, in a way! You learn to respect work and if you ever become a boss, you will know how to appreciate the grunt work and that a country does not rely only on engineers, doctors and teachers!"

After eating, attracted by the pleasant temperature, Elaur took a blanket and the book he had started the night before and went to the nearby plot, where the Great River's pond began. Indeed, on the edge of the shore five or six meters high, the cool wind felt best, so he spread out his blanket and immersed himself in reading.

Two hours had passed, when he noticed that he was no longer alone. More than twenty meters from him, a man with a beard that was still black but with half whitened shoulder-length hair was crouching, looking somewhere in the distance toward the hills beyond the river. He looked like a character taken from the history book, men's long hair but also the rather bushy beard being extremely rare, perhaps because they were not approved by the New Authority.

He could not resist the temptation to approach to see him more closely, especially since the stranger, whom he had never seen before, did not seem to notice him, as he was standing motionless like a statue. He went towards him and spread his blanket about ten meters from him and started to read again. From time to time, looking up from the book, he peeked at the man that was standing still, who seemed to keep his eyes closed. Only when he coughed slowly did the man turn his head slightly in his direction, still keeping his eyes closed, so that he could immediately turn his head back.

His closed eyes intrigued Elaur even more, struggling with his crazy curiosity and desire to get closer but also with an indefinite fear of that man, who was quite big and so strange.

He became brave and, moving a little away from the steep bank, descended into a pit, no deeper than two meters, with an almost truncated cone shape, about ten meters in diameter, which they had called the „Globe of Courage," because they came here on their bicycles, making circular turns on the wall of the pit, inclined at over thirty degrees, without falling, even if the bicycle was much inclined towards its center.

Walking very carefully, he came out of the pit less than three meters away, to his left and slightly behind him. The stranger made no move and they both stood for almost a minute like two living statues, Elaur just turning his gaze and studying where he might flee if the man became threatening. He shuddered slightly when he said in a calm, soothing voice:

„Do you want to talk?"

Elaur hesitated for a second and replied rather cautiously:

„Yes! I really like talking to people! I always have something to learn!"

„Don't be afraid of me! I don't keep my eyes closed, that's how I was born! I am blind since birth! I live there, across the street from this place, in the house of my aunt, who died. Come and sit here on the grass, next to me! My name is Tinu!"

Becoming brave, he approached and sat to the left of the stranger, also introducing himself:

„My name is Elaur! Did anyone bring you here?"

„I have this stick with which I check the road in front of me! It's the fourth day I'm coming here. I have already learned the way! Tell me, this shore, how high is it? At this problem my stick doesn't help me anymore!"

„It is about six meters high and it is almost vertical! You must not get too close!"

The man answered, moving his head slightly up and down:

„Thank you for caring for me," the man told him.

After a minute, in which Elaur studied him continuously, he said:

„Don't be afraid of me! Now, because you were able to look at me, I would like to look at you too! Don't be scared! I have never hurt anyone! Give me your right hand, and please put your left hand on my heart!"

Turning a little toward him, Elaur was in that position which seemed strange and solemn to him at the same time. His palm was lost between the man's large, warm palms, his fingers facing him, feeling their soft skin take over every millimeter of his palm's skin. They stayed like that for more than two minutes, until Elaur wasn't scared at all, feeling an unshakeable peace. Almost whispering, the blind man said to him:

„Elaur, you have to take care of yourself! Your mother's heart is with you all the time. I feel that the source of her tears is almost dry. She lost a child, didn't she?" Without waiting for the boy's confirmation, he continued, in the same warm, almost mysterious voice:

„If you lose yourself, her heart will not resist! You need to know this! You must especially not forget! Now, I want you to think that man can be an incredibly resilient being, but just as well, his life can be like smoke, now it is, and in the blink of an eye, a gust of wind can dispel it!"

After a moment of silence, impressed and slightly frightened by the man's words, agreeing with what the man said about his mother, he replied:

„Thank you for telling me! Now I have to go! Do you want me to help you get home?"

„I can get there by myself! Although it doesn't look like it, I feel the rain is approaching and I have to go too! We can go together to my gate. There are some children who bother me every time."

Elaur went to get his book and the blanket and turning, he took the man's left hand, which had risen slightly and placed it on his right forearm, both of them heading for the road at the edge of the plot, which on the left was getting to the pond and on the right, after about fifty yards, intersected the street parallel to his street, beyond it, being the very house where Tinu lived.

„You see, Elaur, what a strange man I am! I can see things you don't see, but I can't see where I'm stepping! I don't upset anyone, but those your age or younger either avoid me or make fun of me! You'll see right away!"

He could scarcely finish speaking that from the corner of the fence of the first courtyard, which was on the same line as the plot, three boys, five or six years younger than Elaur, rushed around and sang in choir:

„Tinu-the crazy man!, Tinu-the crazy man! Tiinuuu-the crazy man!!"

„I can't do anything abouy them! It's not their fault! If their parents don't take care, what can I do about them?"

Elaur followed them, chasing them to the entrance of a courtyard. He turned and said:

„Mr. Tinu, don't mind them! I know the father of two of them and I'm going to talk to him. I hope it calms them down! Otherwise, I will calm them down with some kicks in the ass! I promise they won't bother you anymore!"

„Thank you so much! Mind your own way now! If they don't get accustomed with me, I'll get accustomed with them!"

Elaur greeted him respectfully, then went home. Tinu's house was somehow placed diagonally to their house and Elaur knew that from that point on, he had the same distance until home, whether he would return to the Mill Street, or go to the street parallel to it. He chose the second option, to pass in front of the court where the three children who were bothering Tinu had taken refuge.

Elaur, who suspected they were alone at home, stopped at the gate, pretending to open the latch inside and said:

„You fools! I'll break your legs if you'll bother Mr. Tinu again!"

He left after they ran away scared into the house. He walked slower than usual, thinking about the strange way Tinu had „looked" at him, but also about what he said, and as some things he couldn't have possibly known.

Chapter 10

As every year, at the beginning of autumn, the Fair was the main joy of the children, a good opportunity for fun for young people, as well as the main shopping period for their parents. Everyone was looking forward to its arrival.

The tradition of the Fair was almost two hundred and fifty years old and its character of annual celebration awaited by all the locals, had consecrated among the inhabitants an interesting expression of solidarity, manifested since ancient times. Thus, the one who selflessly helped a friend or a neighbor, when asked how much the service costed, instead of „It doesn't cost you anything!" he answered, almost invariably: „A beer at the Fair!"

Young or old, nicely dressed, people came at the Fair at least three or four times, between the first and the eighth of September, the busiest days being Sunday and the main day, ie the last day of the Fair, the eighth of September. Despite all the mischief done during the year, when they were warned by their parents, „We won't take you to the Fair this year!", the little ones were forgiven every year and one or both parents, even an older brother or sister, came at the Fair during the day, holding their hand, to enjoy the merry-go-round, the boats and the chains, but also the long-awaited cotton candy, the vanilla donuts and even the handcrafted lollipops. Tired and happy, the little ones returned from the Fair with hats on their heads and blowing loud trumpets, both made of the same colored cardboard, falling asleep early in the evening and dreaming of the enchanted merry-go-round that had taken them over the City.

Also during the day, those interested in various purchases came at the Fair, from where, in addition to clothes and shoes, housewives bought certain fruits, which could be found harder in the plains, pears for compotes, plums for jam and apples for the famous pies. From the Fair they also bought garlic for the winter and various objects for the kitchen, from the sieve to the saucepan or the cauldron, from the wooden trough used for the preparation of the dough, to wooden spoons and beautifully colored ceramic pots.

In their turn, the men chose, also from the craftsmen who came „from the mountains", one a bigger barrel for the sauerkraut, another a new barrel for wine or a bathing tub, which was also a trough, but was made out of the trunk of a thicker tree. In recent years, since they no longer had carts, the people of Miraveda used the indispensable bicycle to transport heavy or bulky goods. At the bicycle they added a two-wheeled cart with a long metal bar.

On Sundays and on the main day, starting around nine or ten o'clock, on the three access roads to the City was organized a real carnival of the carts going to the Fair. They came from all the villages around the city, from nearby or even from twenty to twenty-five kilometers away, beautifully adorned with colored tinsel, most passing right through Miraveda, where children went out on the road to see them. The horses, freshly cleaned and groomed, with their manes and even their tails woven with gold or silver ribbons, looked as if they came from the stories of real princesses and princes. The soundscape was also a special one, the harnesses of the horses being provided with brass bells, of different sizes, which in the slower or more nervous movements of the horses produced small symphonies of joy, transmitting everybody a true festive atmosphere. The high and mighty villagers, nicely dressed and seated in two or three rows in carts, were very proud of their horses and carts, but also of the spectacle offered to those who stopped at the side of the road to watch them.

Adolescents and young people, but also their parents, went for the fun offered by the Fair after sunset, when most of the villagers were already gone back to their villages, lined up and down the Great River, but also others lost in the immensity of the plain, north of it.

Only then did the real fun begin, the three or four large chains, adorned with variously colored light bulbs, spinning dizzyingly and dominating everyone's eyes, creating a kind of almost general bliss. However, the carousels, equally brightly lit, as well as the circuses, the garlands of light bulbs of the restaurant terraces and those of the stalls contributed to the intense atmosphere, creating a sea of lights, which delighted the visitors and helped them forget the difficulties and the troubles of the year.

From the money „earned" by Elaur on vacation, the most part was spent on clothes or shoes, but he always kept some for the Fair, where he was proud, in front of friends, with the money he had earned.

The Fair had passed and after another week, he had started the eighth grade with the same joy and impatience of the recent years, feeling that it was his only chance to achieve his most secret ambitions. He was dreaming, like any pupil who loved literature, to become a famous respected and loved writer, with whom parents and teachers, but also the people of Miraveda to be proud. It was his secret dream, about which he had not spoken to anyone, but which made him more and more ambitious and which kept him from complacency and forbidden temptations.

More optimistic and confident than ever, he had no way of knowing what a great challenge awaited him in the eighth grade, what excruciating turmoil would come over him, confusing him and putting him in a constant confrontation with himself. Until then, exactly on the first day of school, seeing in the schoolyard a girl from the eighth class C whom he knew, he could not refrain and asked her directly what was the name of her colleague, whom he had met at the Bread Center, telling her the last name he knew.

„Aa-haa, she said, shaking her head slightly. Those days are over," she said, laughing and looking at him knowingly.

„What days?! I don't understand anything!"

„Uca, isn't it? Is she the girl you're asking about?"

„You might be thinking about her, because she blossomed so much this summer! If so, I'm sorry about your heart, but I don't think you've heard the best news!"

„Wait! Why are you confusing me like that? What heart and what news?"

„Well, my dear, you should find out that the beautiful Uca got... ma-rried!"

Elaur looked at her in disbelief for a moment, then asked, slightly puzzled:

„Come on, girl! Are you making fun of me? How could she get married?"

„As you heard! She's been married for exactly three days. She ran away with a tractor driver, but I think her mother forced her! This tractor driver is twenty seven years old, he's thirteen years older than her, but he has his house in Miraveda and enough money. The day before, I met her and it was obvious that she was upset and that she was crying but she didn't want to tell me anything! I think that's why her mother followed and guarded her all summer! What can I say now? Everyone knows that her mother has no job, as she goes at the Farm for the day labor and her father has been out in the world for over three years, leaving both of them!"

As two more girls appeared, curious to find out what their colleague was talking about with the boy from the A class, Elaur greeted her and left for his class, trying to look indifferent, when in fact he was completely confused. The event at the Bread Center took a new and unexpected turn. He thought that he had judged Uca a little easily, making all sorts of crazy plans. He tried to understand her attitude, not knowing if she expected anything from him or if she was consuming only a small and rebellious pleasure, taking revenge on her mother and maybe even on him, the boy who wouldn't look at her and who had just gotten at the final hour.

He thought of her normal desire, of having her own choice, defeated by her mother's calculation, but also of the madness of that carnal pleasure, like an ephemeral rebellion and an attempt to prove to herself that she could bewilder a boy her age.

He felt his world change more and more quickly, offering him so many new situations and sensations, but also so many unpleasant surprises. He was looking around more closely, trying to understand the rules behind which all sorts of things were happening, which escaped his logic, catching him so unprepared. He was especially trying to understand why Codrus had so much hatred and resentment for him, why Leta's family had moved so abruptly to the country and how he had met the daring but unhappy Uca himself, even before her forced marriage.

On top of all this, he was haunted by a discussion with his father, treated with the utmost respect but which had created, for the first time, a small separation between them. After learning from Martia's brother, who came to visit, that Elaur met all the conditions for admission to the Military High School, with very good grades and with the necessary physical condition to pass the eliminatory physical tests, his father had been delighted by the conditions offered in case of success, already seeing Elaur in the spectacular military student uniform.

„What do you say, son? Would you like to become an officer?"

„You have to like this career, Elaur said cautiously. I don't really know what that means!"

„What do you mean, my son? Would it be bad to become an officer? You have a safe job, a very good payroll, plus state clothing!"

„Dad, it might be fine, I'm not saying no! I need to think about it, to find out what it means!"

He had almost told him that he wanted to go to Number Two Theoretical Lyceum, located at the entrance to the City, three minutes from Miraveda.

„Your uncle told me that if you go to the Military High School and you study hard, you automatically go to the Officers' School. Is it an insignificant thing to study seven years on state money? Food, shelter and clothes - those are provided, plus afterwards you go straight to being paid and it's a good salary, not like mine!"

Elaur felt it was not the best time to continue the discussion and postponed it:

„Okay, Dad! I'm going to think seriously about this. I have all the time!"

He remembered his mother's advice, „When you want something, you tell me first because if you tell his father and he says no, then it's hard for me to make him change his mind! Tell me what you want and then I bring your father to the plan!" After telling his mother that he wanted to go to the Theoretical Lyceum and then take the college exam, about two days later his father caught him alone again:

„I understood from your mother that you want to go to the theoretical! If you want to go here in the City, why not at least go to the economical school? From there you come out an accountant, what are you going to be after the theoretical? Come on, tell me what are you going to be, because I didn't find out what!"

In the absence of his mother, Elaur did not want to continue, but his father did not let him out of his sight, waiting for the answer to the question:

„After high school, I take an exam at the college, in the Capital!"

„Oh, boy! Do you think anyone goes to college? That's where the children of the important people go! I even heard that some give a lot of money to be accepted! It's your job! You and your mother decided that, so ask her for money from now on!"

Elaur was silent, thinking he had to talk to his mother again, but he felt he would have to confront his father. After three or four days, one evening, coming from the City, he entered the house without being heard. His parents were arguing in their bedroom. He heard his father's voice:

„You're the one who encouraged Elaur to go to the Theoretical Lyceum! Four years of high school! Let's just say he goes to college. Another four or five years, a total of eight or nine years. Have you ever thought how are we going to be able to keep him in school? We also have Minela!"

„Come on, honey! God is good, he won't leave us," Martia replied.

Elaur had heard his parents tell each other „honey" quietly, but not in the presence of their children. He felt it was a good sign that they weren't even arguing because of him. Tramian continued:

„We'll also have Alena's wedding. Do you know what a girl's wedding means? You spend a lot of money and after the wedding the money raised from the gifts is taken by the father-in-law. If he wants to give something to the young people, alright, if not, he says that he didn't recover his expense and I feel that we also have to help them!"

„You're right, I have nothing to say! But God is great and He helps us! Who gave me this job with the wallpaper if not God? He made me think of wallpaper and He also taught me how to do it!"

„Let's see how it goes! You are at the beginning! If you're gonna have to go back to gluing clay houses I'm not letting you! You've ruined your health enough and you've also put rheumatism in your bones!"

„Look, next week I have two more wallpaper rooms! It's starting to be fashionable! The customers will come little by little"

„Alright honey, but you don't have to ruin yourself because of work either. My soul hurts when I see you so tired. The children know their stuff and we know ours!"

„I'll eat dirt from under my feet and keep Elaur in high school and in college! How many parents wouldn't want to have a boy like him? He is my gratitude and pride!"

Elaur, who was standing at the end of the hall, had tears in his eyes and a lump in his throat. He waited a few seconds then closed the front door loudly and turned on the light on the hall.

„Elaur, is that you, my boy? You see, I left food for you in the kitchen. Don't go to bed without eating!"

He cleared his throat and nodded with a „Yes, Mom!" that still came out a little choked with emotion. He went to his room and turned on the light, sitting at the table where he usually did his homework, with his elbows on the table and his cheeks in his palms. He stood like that for a few minutes, understanding for the first time his father's concern. He even thought it was better to follow his advice and go to the Military High School when there was a knock on the door and he heard Martia's voice:

„Can I come in?"

After he said „yes", Martia entered the room, while Elaur quickly picked up a book from the table, pretending to read from it:

„Come on, I'll give you something to eat! With your reading, you forget about food!"

They both went into the winter kitchen and Martia took a kitchen towel and a smaller plate, placed as a lid, from above the plate of chicken pilaf. She had come to make sure that Elaur ate the pilaf prepared for him, but also to talk to him.

„Maybe I'd better go to the Military High School!"

„Spare me with the Military High School! You go where you want! I really want you here in the City, close to me! I know it would be easier for your father if the state payed but your mother won't let go for seven years in the army for that! And then, to stay and listen to the orders your entire life? I saw that at my brother!"

Raising his eyes from the plate, Elaur saw his mother's shining eyes and looking at her red hands, slightly scorched by lime, with clenched fists that left no room for compassion, he felt like a small child in front of the mountain of will in front of him. Martia watched him eat, to wash over him with her love, to which she always added her love for Nion, her first baby.

„I met Mrs. Parvu, your math teacher, in front of the dispensary, in the bus station. She told me that it's a very good thing that you want to go to High School number two, because they have the best teachers. She praised you in front of everyone waiting the bus and told me that you will enter high school with a high score and you will succeed at the college test. I left that place so happy that there was no one like me! I don't even know how I got home!"

A few months earlier, Martia had found something new and promising, to earn the money so necessary for her ambitions, to help her children as much as possible. At the end of spring, she had been with Tramian to a monastery near the Capital, to pray to a saint, who had been a monk some years earlier at that very monastery and taking advantage of the opportunity, she also passed by an aunt, who lived on the outskirts of the Capital. She was just painting her house, small but well-kept, consisting of two rooms and a hall, plus a kitchen added later, accessible from the hall. Watching the woman painting her walls, who applied a beautiful pattern in one of the rooms, she thought it couldn't be that hard and she'd be able to handle that pattern. The walls were painted in pale green and that woman had two templates, about sixty inches wide and ninety high, one for green and the other for white.

Passing with a brush soaked in a small basin of green paint, over that cut-out template, she applied small segments on the walls of the room, representing some equally small branches and leaves around them, moving the template to the right, but also down, until it covered the whole wall. After finishing the four green walls, she took a tray, put white oxide in it, soaked it in some milk and took the other template. She placed it after some dots, drawn through the first template and with the white brush, she began to apply some white flowers, which blended perfectly with the green branches and leaves, covering the wall with a two-tone carpet.

„You want to steal my job, if you follow me so closely, said that foreign woman, making Martia smile, embarrassed:"

„I live in Miraveda, more than a hundred kilometers from here, but I would love to put such wallpaper in my house!"

The painter woman smiled peacefully at her, saying:

"I don't have enough hands for how much work I have here! I think that in this Capital might be ten like me and we still wouldn't be able to cope!"

"Can these templates be bought? Where do you get them from?"

Martia became brave, she took an empty box of red iron oxide in her hand and studied it more closely.

"I do not know! I got them from an old painter! It didn't cost me anything and if you want, I'll pull them out on some cardboard and cut them at home, because that's how I make new ones when they break! I have three models, if you really want me to make them, you need six pieces of cardboard from a bookstore!"

At Martia's urging, Tramian took their uncle's bicycle and in twenty minutes returned with six sheets of cardboard which the benevolent woman printed in green paint the three wallpaper patterns she had, two for each model.

"After cutting them with a razor blade, you paint them on both sides, two days in a row, with oil paint so that they do not get wet and break. You see that they have some dots in the corners that help you join them! These three are for white and you make their pairs as you like, with green, maroon or blue. Make the wall the same color, but lighter, adding to the lime oxide of the color you choose.

You see that this oxide is soaked only in milk, so it doesn't come off the wall!"

Martia had taken some money out of her pocket to reward her but as the woman refused, looking at her sympathetically, she hugged and kissed her on both cheeks:

"May God reward you, woman! Let Him give to you according to your good soul," Martia told her.

Arriving in Miraveda, she whitewashed Elaur's room four times, placing the respective wallpapers, one pattern on each wall, then covering them with cream lime, to start over, over and over again, until she learned not only the secret of the wallpaper, but also how much he had to soak the brush in oxide, so as not to drip under the template.

Tramian, impressed by Martia's will and skill, didn't stand idle either and from a vinyl notebook cover, he had cut a piece twenty centimeters by seven and with the same blade he cut out a small pattern for drawing straight lines, as he had seen at the woman in the Capital. He had also payed attention to everything he had seen at the woman who had given them the models, he took a cotton thread, rolled it through the red oxide powder, stretched it between two points, helped by Martia. Then he pinched the well stretched thread so that the oxide passed from the thread to the wall, thus appearing a thin and perfectly straight line. Along this thin line, with the line template and a small brush dipped in oxide dissolved in milk, he had drawn the desired line along the entire length of the wall.

After learning them well, Martia put all three wallpaper patterns in three different rooms to "sample" them, as she said and present them to those interested and Tramian had drawn the lines, fifteen centimeters from the ceiling and five centimeters from the corners. In the end, tired and with dirty hands, clothes and face, after looking excitedly at the result, they looked confident and worshipped the Lord for the new skill they had learned.

Chapter 11

Elaur had learned more details from his neighbors about high school admission, which began with two written tests in math and literature, followed by three oral tests in the same two subjects, plus national history. He was quite confident, especially after talking to Elu, his neighbor, who was in his senior year at the very high school where he also wanted to be admitted:

„As far as I know, you have no problems with literature and math! If you swot some history, you can be admitted on the first half of the list."

Elaur had learned that, every year, the competition for admission was almost three candidates for one place, and he was a little bit afraid of history, although he found it captivating, because of his modest ability to memorize numbers, he feared that he would not be able to remember the innumerable data of historical events. Instead, he had a good memory of facts and situations, recounting various events or readings from the past, with details that most people did not notice or remember. The faces of the interlocutors, especially of those who interested him for one reason or another, were just as easily imprinted in his mind, easily reconstituting them in his mind, even after many years.

Like a blind man that would sharpen his other senses, Elaur had developed the ability to do calculations quickly, even mentally, but after a few hours, if you asked him the result, he would rather remember the calculation than remember the result. In order to remember certain numbers, he had discovered an ingenious method of associating his numbers with the words of a small sentence, each word having a number of letters equal to the number it replaced.

Beyond the small worries about the first exam in his life in the eighth grade, the biology textbook had triggered a real storm in his mind and soul, so he read it in its entirety, from the first weeks of school and he even re-read carefully certain pages. Moreover, he had obtained a more complex book of biology, for the fourth year of high school, the readings on species variability, heredity and natural selection, the foundations of the theory of evolution, provoking unexpected revelations, but also qualms of conscience, feeling how he slipped, little by little, into another world than the one in which he had grown up.

From the simple world, created by God in seven days, in which the line between good and evil was very clearly defined, willingly or not, he passed into a new world, in which all sorts of questions were asked and in which appeared so many doubts. It is true that there were answers, but if some were satisfactory, others seemed rather incomplete, even contradictory, as those managed not only to confuse him, but to cause him excruciating turmoil. He had had a fairly applied but sincere and gentle religious upbringing, so that in the first seven years of school he had found no difficulty in obeying his fatherțs earnest urge to follow his faith without talking too much with others about it.

God's denial was felt by Elaur as a capital sin, as he wouldn't dare to oppose even a fleeting thought to the faith with which he had grown. Moreover, he felt that his desire to understand what was written in biology books and the questions he sometimes asked himself, even if they did not deny the existence of divinity, were also unforgivable sins.

„The devil tempts you, especially through evil desires and thoughts! In his great cunning, he can also change the face of science and then use it to divert people from the right path," Tramian had told him at some point.

His father, after many and deep religious readings, had acquired a certain language, so he surprised all those who knew that he had only graduated the fourth grade, with the information he had, but also with the fluency of his speech.

„Teachers, most of them for fear of losing their jobs and others, maddened by the work of the Evil One, put all kinds of lies in your head, wanting to convince you of a great foolishness, that man had evolved from the ape and not that he is the Perfect Work of God. They are now laughing at the holy things, but they will come to account at the Last Judgment!"

Elaur, who had finished his math homework, listened intently to his father, who had just closed the Bible, trying to understand if his words were incidentally referring to his great turmoil, or were specially chosen, as he was feeling his inner turmoil. He didn't answer, knowing that his father did not expect such a thing either, as he liked the calm tone and the unexpected level of what he had said. Tramian had somehow felt, or perhaps he had even been warned by the priest about the danger in Elaur's books and was looking his son in the eye expecting from him only attention and good faith, not forced confirmations or false speeches. For a few weeks, Elaur managed to crush the conflict within him, as he spent his time reading books from the exam curriculum, but also with many math problems, from a specially purchased collection. He had borrowed two of the necessary books from the school library and when he went to return them he met Lexia, whom he had only seen two or three times from a great distance, disappearing quite quickly.

As always, she was dressed in a certain way, wearing a pale pink dress, with faded cherry puff sleeves, with a wide cord, the color of the sleeves, tied in a double bow on the left side. This time, looking at her closely, it seemed to Elaur that their age difference could not be more than a year, maximum two. For her part, Lexia stopped to look at him more closely, analysing him up and down:

„You've grown quite a bit since we last spoke, but I see that your passion for reading has also grown. Let's see what books you have there!"

Elaur answered, showing her the books:

„Mandatory reading for the summer exam. I wanted to read them before we got to study them in class, but I really liked them."

As he talked to her, Elaur looked at her delicate hands, with very white skin, almost translucent. He was embarrassed that he was sweating after the football game, which was organized in the school yard. Without looking embarrassed in any way, Lexia put her right hand on his shoulder, asking him almost in a whisper:

„Do you want to go to a special meeting tomorrow night after school? You will meet some special people, as you do not often have the opportunity to meet elsewhere!”

„I finish classes at ten to seven! Where do I have to come?”

„Do you know that big house on the opposite side of the grocery store? It is right on the corner, it has two columns at the entrance which support a triangular frontispiece and is painted yellow!”

„I know it very well! Like any man in Miraveda, I guess! At what time am I supposed to come?”

He looked at her puzzled, knowing that house was deserted, but he was determined to go there, as she not only inspired him confidence, but he felt a state of grace around her, that was hard to describe in words.

„You come straight from school! I'll be there! Don't go inside without me!”

He nodded and after Lexia, taking her hand from his shoulder, waved her long, thin fingers in farewell, he entered the library, quite surprised by her proposal.

The state of provocation and slight confusion he felt in her presence had nothing of the thrill of feelings for Leta two years earlier, much less the dazzling attraction he had felt for Uca.

The next day, at school, he eagerly awaited the meeting proposed by Lexia, trying to understand what people he was to meet. He was dressed in his uniform, as on any other day, but he had taken a blue shirt, which he had ironed himself, the two white shirts on his hangers looking a little dull. He had put on blue socks and a pair of black shoes, almost new, not forgetting to let his mother know that he would be late, having some activity at school.

Immediately after the bell announced the end of the last class, Elaur closed his rather large bag, asking Lefan to take it home. Having freed his hands, he sprinted to the road, which he reached in two minutes, then walked at the same speed to the grocery store, already seeing Lexia on the other side of the street. He crossed the road cautiously, first waiting for an old, noisy blue truck to pass, during this time he noticed that Lexia had respect for herself, being dressed just as elegantly. This time, she was dressed in a milky coffee-colored two-piece suit with a rather tight skirt, above the knees and a very elegant coat, but with a cut reminiscent of the thirties, unbuttoned, revealing a cream blouse, knitted compactly, with a rather sober pattern. The high ankle boots, with matching heels and braided up laces, made her look taller, giving her an almost princely look.

„Good evening! I came as fast as I could! I hope I'm not late!"

„Punctuality is a gesture of nobility, she replied, but as long as we have not set an exact time, there is no need to worry. You arrived quite on time!"

She made a sign for him to follow her, they went on the street that was perpendicular to the road, so that after more than ten meters, opening a secondary gate, of which Elaur had no idea, they would enter the courtyard, right behind the house. Elaur followed her on the sidewalk built next to the wall of the house, not more than a meter wide and which continued at a right angle, after the other corner of the house, with a double width.

The part of the house near the road was wider, more than three meters on both sides, and the vestibule, open to the road, was built as wide as the back side, giving the house a cross-shaped section, designed specifically by the architect or perhaps requested by its first owner. After climbing three steps to a large oak door, Lexia applied three light strokes with her finger in the slightly blackened wood, with small pauses between them and immediately a young man gently opened the door and after seeing Lexia, he let them in.

„Good evening, Sofian! Thanks for the promptness!"

„Hi, Lexia! I was in the hallway. You arrived just on time! The debate begins immediately!"

It was already dark when they entered a hall paved with cappuccino marble, dimly lit by an oil lamp, much larger than the ones he knew from the market, as it had a pink marble oil tank, with diffuse gray lines, the metal part was made from brass and it also had an unusually large and very clean glass. The man, who was not more than thirty years old, followed by Lexia, headed to the staircase at the end of the hall, covered with white marble, probably to visually mark the steps and to add brightness to the area. With a handrail of yellow metal, probably still brass, the staircase was leading down, in a tight spiral, to a high basement, where the light of another lamp, identical to the one in the hall, awaited them.

In front of them was a room seven meters wide and nine meters long, having at the end of the stairs a kind of hardwood stage, across the width of the room, sixty centimeters high, with three narrow steps on the right side. On the stage was placed a vintage table, slightly oval and six chairs, matching the table, four of which were behind the table, facing the hall and the other two at its ends.

In front of the stage were placed three rows of four upholstered chairs, having the same shape as those on the stage, but slightly smaller and with the upholstery of a different color. For better visibility, the seats in the second row were put a little bit to the left, next to the free spaces between the seats in front of them.

At the top of the wall next to the courtyard the room had two rectangular vents, twenty inches above the sidewalk, on either side of the steps in front of the oak door. Protected by stylized bars, of the same wrought iron, over which were applied metal screens with small meshes, they made the air in the room unexpectedly fresh. After Sofian went on the stage, sitting in one of the chairs at the end of the table, Lexia whispered to Elaur:

„Please sit on one of the chairs in the room! I'll stay here in the back, on the couch."

Elaur sat in the only free chair in row three on the left, discreetly studying the faces of the other eight people in the auditorium, of which only two boys and a girl were his age, two girls in their senior year in high school and three men in their thirties. On the table were placed two lamps identical to those placed in the hallway and next to the stairs, somehow illuminating the room, but also giving it an austere and mysterious air. After two or three minutes, going down the stairs, a lady appeared. She was about forty-five, with almost white hair, caught in a very elaborate bun, giving her an air of great distinction and the allure of a demanding teacher. Elaur's attention was immediately caught by the young man who was coming after her and who was none other than Favian, the boy from the Capital, who had taught him poker two years ago.

Elaur's surprise increased even more when he went on stage and after the white-haired lady sat in a chair facing the hall, he also sat in the chair at the other end of the table, opposite the one occupied by Sofian. He was wearing quite new blue jeans, a white turtleneck with a collar wrapped around his neck and a black leather jacket, in obvious opposition to the blue suit and the white shirt with which Sofian had come, but also to the sober dress of the lady, made of gray knitted wool, accessorized with a white scarf, fastened in front with a silver brooch, on which was mounted a black stone.

„Good evening my dears! My name is Vera, I have a degree in philosophy and theology and I will be your host tonight!"

Her warm, almost melodious voice contrasted with the first impression she had left, of a demanding and distant teacher.

„We invited to this discussion our young friends, Mr. Sofian, a graduate in philosophy and Mr. Favian, a recent graduate of the Institute of Physical Education and Sports. Let's hope that we all leave here with richer ideas and more confident in our options. In all our endeavors, we will not say or do anything against the authorities or against any private person, but my request is that, once you leave here, you show discretion, being the only attitude that is good for everyone, for those present here, but also for society in general! The topic of our discussion is „Philosophical Ethics and Christian Moral" and the level of approach will be quite accessible."

Chapter 12

"We will begin our debate with the presentation of the philosophical concept of morality. Please, Mr. Sofian, said Mrs. Vera."

Placing the sheets in front of him, more out of habit than to look at them, he began his presentation:

"Because morality has an indisputable practical purpose, beyond theoretical considerations, we will start from a very short and as simple as possible definition and then develop our presentation, using some of its important features. Therefore, morality is a system of social behavior, which imposes the character of the thoughts, decisions and deeds of those who share it and want to respect it. It reflects the level of development of society and applies to all, even those who do not know it, or who do not recognize it, as it has a certain imperative character, given not by law, but by public opinion."

Sofian was speaking slowly, with short pauses after each sentence, continuing in the same way:

"Morality is the main means of promoting the social good and the generally accepted norms of conduct, likely to facilitate a harmonious coexistence between members of society. For this, morality has the role of controling certain human impulses that are socially unacceptable and related to the moods generated by the desires for power, well-being, sex, etc... Moreover, morality imposes an emotional, psychic and even spiritual state, of harmonizing the individual good with the general one, facilitating the power of the individual to bear the fear and the dangers that arise during the fight to eliminate evil from society."

"Thank you, Mr. Sofian, for this presentation and especially for its concreteness and clarity!"

"Mr. Favian, do you want to add anything?"

He had listened to the presentation, looking more at the two girls in their senior year of high school than at Sofian and, a little surprised by Mrs. Vera's question, he turned slightly to her and began in an agitated tone:

"Morality is very good, but only when it is imposed by moral people! In my life I have met many people who demanded the respect of morality, without them respecting it! No offense, I'm kind of fed up with so much morality, rammed down my throat!"

He looked briefly at Mrs. Vera, obviously surprised by his point blank style, continuing:

"As Sofian said, the practical character must be taken into account, because the young people are a little tired of theory!"

Mrs. Vera looked at him indulgently and in the same warm, benevolent tone, she said to him:

"Thank you, Mr. Favian, for the opinion that was so sincerely expressed! As I promise you that we will also address the practical aspects of our subject, I want to show you now the other side of morality, namely, Christian morality. Morality as defined by Mr. Sofian, which we will hereafter call, for differentiation, philosophical ethics, has many things in common with Christian morality, but the latter has in addition features and norms of conduct that make it clearly superior, in my opinion. In addition to the rules relating to the duty towards our neighbor and the practical reasons for guiding the good coexistence, there is a very special concept in Christian morality, that of Christian love, which removes any form of selfishness from the human soul, and it brings into the souls of those who practice it a form of absolute happiness, unknown to others. Christian love is manifested towards others, but also towards God, who represents the Great Goodness!"

After a few moments, as she looked at those in front of her, Mrs. Vera continued:

"While philosophical ethics starts from happiness, as the goal of human life on earth, Christian morality proposes happiness to be the goal of human life too, but it also proposes the perfection of the human being and the attainment of salvation, which begins here on Earth and continues in the afterlife. A good example of the incapacity of philosophical ethics to impose generally valid moral norms is given by the philosophical schools of Greco-Roman antiquity, founded and promoted by the luminaries of those times, Heraclitus, Socrates, Plato and Aristotle. These schools had only a limited influence, the followers and even their founders, hardly complying with the stated norms."

Sofian, who had listened very carefully to what Mrs. Vera said, receiving her discreet consent, intervened:

"However, when we talk about the philosophical schools of Greco-Roman antiquity, we cannot stop only at their influence among the people of those times, as long as the entire European civilization was built on the foundations of Greco-Roman culture and civilization. Its influence and therefore the influence of the philosophical schools you have mentioned, has been felt continuously over the past two millennia and it has decisively determined culture and science, as we know them today."

Looking at him with great interest, Mrs. Vera asked him in the same warm voice:

"And what was, after all, the binder of the European civilization? Wasn't that Christianity?"

"Without question, but in time Christianity has also taken many of the ethical norms of ancient philosophy, which denotes an evolution over time of the concept of morality, a good example being even Christian morality, which is a spiritual development of philosophical ethics as this, in turn, did not appear out of nowhere, being a development and sublimation of older moral systems."

Mrs. Vera replied in the same equal voice:

"Let us not forget, however, that Christian morality is based on the teaching of Christ, by relating to an Absolute Being, identical with the Great Goodness, which is God, undoubtedly surpassing philosophical ethics, based on human reason."

"Mr. Favian, if you have any theoretical considerations to make, please!"

Noticing the unfavorable reaction of those in the room, including the two girls, to his first intervention, he imposed a calmer tone and a more theoretical approach:

"Mrs. Vera, you spoke a little earlier about removing any form of selfishness from the human soul, but throughout human history, it is precisely this selfish side of man, namely the instinct for conservation, that has led to the perpetuation of the human species, to the progress of society, and to material well-being."

As he saw the positive reaction of the girls, he felt encouraged:

"As long as an individual, respecting the law and freedom of others, builds a certain personal comfort, his happiness violates neither philosophical ethics nor Christian morality! I really don't think we all have to live like hermits to get to heaven!"

Mrs. Vera smiled kindly, looking at Favian, then at Sofian, who, accepting the discipline of dialogue, was waiting for his turn:

"Mr. Sofian, you are much closer to the age of Mr. Favian and to the age of all our guests in the room. Can you comment on this point of view, which is extremely interesting?"

"I don't think that superimposing selfishness on the self-preservation instinct is the most inspired solution, especially since selfishness has almost exclusively social connotations and the self-preservation instinct refers especially to the challenges and dangers of the environment, being common to all living beings."

Favian intervened immediately, visibly irritated:

"But if an individual attacks you on the street to rob you, then doesn't your conservation instinct come into play?"

"That's exactly what I was going to say, Sofian replied very calmly. It is obvious that self-defense, in front of the aggressions of others, violates neither philosophical ethics, nor Christian morality, nor the law, if it is not disproportionate, being the concept of legitimate defense."

"What do you mean by disproportionate self-defense?"

Sofian, too little bothered by Favian's impulsive style, replied calmly:

"Self-defense involves the elimination of danger, even by violent means, seeking the defense of one's life and not the physical elimination of the aggressor. Not even its subsequent punishment is acceptable, for that there are laws, which are applied by the state authorities."

Feeling that Sofian was slightly distracted from his analysis, Mrs. Vera felt compelled to intervene:

"Mr. Favian, your position is now more theoretical! Turning to the practical aspects, which you love, don't you think that precisely because of the non-violation of philosophical ethics and Christian morality, to which you referred, we should first know and even understand them? And I'm not necessarily referring to you, but to the young people you talked about earlier who were tired of theory! I see, here in the hall, young people, some even very young, eager to understand both the theoretical concepts and their practical aspects."

"With all due respect! The young people I was referring to are different from those in the room, selected by you. They want clear and certain things, not theoretical definitions and debates!"

Receiving Mrs. Vera's consent to intervene, the peaceful Sofian, feeling he was losing his Socratic patience, tried to temper the impulsive Favian:

"We were also selected by Mrs. Vera! I don't know by which criteria, but I'm starting to understand!"

He continued to the room, immediately giving up the sarcastic tone:

"There is nothing reprehensible in believing that we can have practical "clear and safe" solutions, all the time and for all the problems, without resorting to theoretical concepts, crystallized in thousands of years!"

Although Sofian wanted to continue, Favian, with a rather disturbed face, intervened:

"And I don't think I was selected to receive all kinds of corrections! It could be unpleasant for everyone!"

Mrs. Vera, making a discreet sign to Sofian to wait, intervened peacefully:

"No one is here to receive corrections and I don't think anything like that has happened! We wanted a debate of ideas and we really had it. It is important to understand the role of such debates, attacking the ideas we do not agree with and not those who issue them! Mr. Sofian, please!"

He looked calmly at Favian, trying to bring the conversation on a peaceful path.

"That's unquestionable! I just wanted to express my opinion and even regret, that most of the time there are no clear things and even less certain, no matter how desirable this is! Moreover, I believe that philosophical ethics and Christian morality must intervene exactly where things are not clear and especially when they are not certain! I apologize if I was understood differently!"

"There is no need to apologize, Favian immediately teased him, intentionally ignoring the elegance of Sofian's position. In the end, we have to remain friends, thanking Mrs. Vera, for giving us the opportunity to express our principles!"

Seeing that Sofian was no longer going to enter Favian's hypocritical game, Mrs. Vera addressed all those present:

"We end our debate here, thanking you for your attention! Thank you, Mr. Favian! Thank you Mr. Sofian! For the next debate you will be contacted by our friend, Lexia! I also thank her from the bottom of my heart, for making these debates possible! Good evening everyone!"

Leaving with Mrs. Vera, Favian discreetly winked at Elaur, in recognition, walking to the marble staircase very confidently, looking victorious. Elaur left with Lexia, and when they felt the pleasant evening air, she said to him:

"I hope you enjoyed the debate and that you will come to others! It seemed to me that you know Favian. Is it true?"

"Yes, we met two years ago! I learned to play poker from him, Elaur replied, slightly confused."

"What did you learn? Poker? I didn't know he also taught poker lessons!"

Elaur looked at her intently, not knowing if her irony was only about Favian or about him, and chose to talk about the debate, the subject of which had surprised him quite a bit:

"I really liked the debate, but I didn't quite understand what Favian was doing at that table. Not only did he not rise to the occasion, but his argumentation was rather grumpy than well-founded!"

"I think Mrs. Vera did very well to invite him. He is a successful young man, already adored by many girls in the City and very popular among young people. Mrs. Vera met him at a relative of hers in the City and considered that, for the diversity of opinions, he is welcome to the debate."

"There would be another problem, a bit difficult to solve! I don't understand when he graduated the Institute of Physical Education as I don't really get the calculation, with his years of studies!"

Lexia smiled, surprised by Elaur's problem.

"That's my fault! I told Mrs. Vera that he was a physical education teacher and she assumed that he had graduated from the Institute of Physical Education and Sports. With all the trouble that the New Authority has given her, her good soul and faith in people will never change. In fact, Favian finished high school this summer, in the Capital, and at the beginning of the school year he became substitute physical education teacher, at a school in the City. We both know that education matters, but we also know that certain people can overcome their condition. Favian is an opinion leader in his group and that qualified him for the debate."

"I think you are right! Maybe without Favian's interventions, the subject would have seemed more boring! I really liked the way Mrs. Vera and especially Mr. Sofian responded."

"It is an unwritten rule in these debates, to invite people with as diverse opinions as possible. Mrs. Vera, although no one can shake her beliefs, does not like to listen to opinions that are different from hers, especially from young people."

As they arrived at the bus station from the Mill, Lexia informed Elaur that she was going to wait the bus for the City. He smiled and said:

"No problem! We will wait together! I live nearby, but I don't want to leave you alone until the bus arrives! If you let me know in advance, I really want to not miss any debate!"

They waited together more than half an hour, during which time they talked about books and writers, of which Elaur had barely heard, as she kept talking to him about the books he shouldn't miss, and he kept looking at her as if she was a mysterious being which came from another planet.

Chapter 13

Elaur's parents preferred not to relate in any way to the New Authority, although their words sometimes showed dissatisfaction with the difficulties of procuring the necessaries of life, but also with its attitude, so hostile to the church.

"The bread they give us, not only is it on the card, but it also looks as if from year to year it is darker in color and worse in taste, Martia often complained."

Three or four years earlier, however, Elaur had heard her scold her middle brother, who, whenever he drank an extra peg, began to swear at the representative of the New Authority at Calavechi:

"That damn cracker, he has only BS in his head. The bum of the village came to lead and to teach us, to be fair and to love the New Authority! Let him love it, because he has built that big house! From what? They were the poorest in the village and now they have become the richest! The damn traitor, how easy it is for him to work with his mouth!"

Martia looked around in fright and whispered to him:

"Hey, little brother! Take it easy with these words! Can you hear what you're saying? At least talk only about him! Stop taking on the New Authority! You have two children who need a father! Do you want them to take you, like Titus's, who would swear at them in the pub until they arrested him? It's been over fifteen years since then and no one knows about him. Not where he is, not even if he's still alive!"

When she saw Elaur beside them, she changed the subject, making a sign for her brother to be silent.

A year earlier, in the seventh grade, it was Elaur's turn to be a member of the New Youth Authority, and his parents did not object, since all pupils became members by the end of the eighth grade, when even the worst were admitted. Tramian did not like what the New Youth Authority taught children, especially about religion and the church, but he agreed with Martia, who had said to him from the beginning:

"Let the child go with his classmates! Those are different things! It matters what he has in his soul, not what they tell him there! Let's not rebel to hurt the boy!"

Initially, neither Elaur nor Arian, the best in his class, were among the first five pupils in their class to be accepted into the New Youth Authority. Instead, his colleague and cousin, Mira, a gentle and obedient girl, immediately after the acceptance, had been elected to the NYA School Bureau and assistant secretary. The school secretary, Anet, a girl Elaur barely knew, was from the seventh C grade.

"Your time will come, said the teacher who coordinated the NYA school organization. You have to prepare very well! Take the status from your colleague Mira and learn it by heart. By the end of the seventh grade, we need to gather ten more members!"

Concerned with other things, Elaur had studied the aforementioned status at the beginning of the third term, just the night before that meeting, when he had been received in the organization, together with Arian, the head of the class. This was after, a few days before, a colleague, who lived near the church in Miraveda, had said to him, grinning:

"What do you say, Elaur, if I go to the NYA and tell them I saw you at the Easter service surrounding the church with your sister and your father, with lit candles in your hands?"

Elaur frowned at him, but he immediately had an indifferent expression and he said:

"Go ahead! I couldn't care less! They will accept me anyway in the eighth grade, when they accept even suckers like you!"

He really wouldn't have lost anything by the end of seventh grade, except for two boring meetings and paying the mandatory dues. In the eighth grade, however, upset by his indifference, Anet could not lose sight of him:

"Elaur, you have all kinds of achievements, but at the NYA I don't really see you in the first row. I want us to talk, to see how you can improve your political activity! Until then, you could, for example, help your cashier collect the dues. You are the first in class, but you are the last to pay the NYA dues!"

Elaur smiled, looking away, especially because he remembered that he was not up to date with the dues, and said:

"You'd better give me another task! Luxa does not need help with collecting taxes. She's able to chase us in the class to pay her that money! You'd better give me another task!"

"Good! I'll think of a more interesting task. Tonight, after school, come to the NYA office, because we have an office meeting! You're invited!"

Not very pleased with the school secretary's interest in him, but somewhat curious to see what an office meeting looked like, at nine o'clock he was present in the room on the ground floor of the school, located just below the teachers' room, where the members of the bureau had already gathered, a representative of the four eighth grades, two seventh grade pupils and Anet.

"I think you all know Elaur, who is the guest of our meeting today."

He noticed immediately that in the said office the girls dominated, there were only two boys, both from the eighth grade, good boys, but a bit dull and dominated by the authoritarian Anet. After each topic discussed, apart from those who spoke, she took care to invite him to share his opinion! Before the end of the meeting, she announced, very seriously:

"For the school General Assembly, after the opening of the works, Elaur will have a presentation, entitled 'Combating religious obscurantism, a permanent task of the New Youth Authority'!"

Elaur, thinking he missunderstood something, looked at Anet in astonishment, understanding that it was about him, only after seeing the crooked smile of his cousin, who knew that his father had recently accepted the position of psalm reader at the church in Miraveda, after the old one, a graduate of the psalm readers school, had retired due to the illness that had pinned him to bed.

After the meeting, he waited a few minutes, until he and Anet were alone, addressing her quite bewildered:

"I don't want you to think I'm running away from work, especially since I asked you to give me another task!"

Anet did not let him continue, answering immediately:

"Come on, Elaur! You're a smart boy! I think you will have a very good presentation!"

He looked at her and did not know how to continue:

"Not that I couldn't write this presentation, but I have a problem with my father. He is very faithful, he has been going to church since he was a child and because he learned the religious service by heart, the priest chose him to be a psalm reader, here at the church in Miraveda. I don't want to upset him and I don't think it's good idea for the NYA to let me present this topic!"

Anet looked at him a little confused:

"Look, I didn't think of that! It's damn complicated! I have already announced in the Office and I have also spoken with the tutor! After all, only a few know that your father is a psalm reader and he can't hear about your presentation!"

Elaur looked at her thoughtfully, without saying anything more, when Anet said to him:

"Let's go! It's late and the cleaning lady is waiting for us to leave so she can lock the school! I'll find a solution in the end!"

They both went out the teachers' door and headed to the road, as she asked him to accompany her, because Anet lived on the other side of Miraveda, across the road. After they left the school yard, at some point, Anet said to him:

"I don't know what to say to our tutor! I don't want to tell him about your father, but I can't find any other excuse, especially since he was delighted when I proposed to you!"

They were close to the road, passing a house whose back wall had remained right on the street, after the last widening of the streets in Miraveda. Suddenly, Elaur felt two strong arms that grabbed him by force from behind, twisted him to the right and pushed him facing the wall. Instinctively, he turned his head too, to the right, to avoid hitting his face against the wall and only then did he recognize Codrus's red, grim face.

"What the hell are you doing with Anet?!"

He pushed him slightly to his left, at the corner of the rough plastered wall of the house, with a chimney of burnt brick, glued to the wall and plastered just like it. He twisted his right hand so hard that Elaur gasped in pain, already immobilizing him and holding him with only his left hand, still twisting his hand and pushing him hard into that angle. Anet, barely recovering from the surprise of Codrus's attack, saw the knife he had taken out with his right hand and put at Elaur's throat. She immediately uttered a frightened "Nooo..." and approached the two fearfully:

"Please leave him alone! I'm to blame, she said in horror, crying and stroking Codrus on the shoulder of his left hand, with which he was holding Elaur. I asked him to come with me! I was afraid to walk alone! Can't you see how dark it is? I'm begging you! Pleeeaaase!"

Elaur, who had felt the cold blade of the knife at his throat, without seeing or understanding what it was, was just as terrified anyway. Anet, who seemed to know Codrus well, continued to beg him, weeping:

"Please! Pleease! If I knew you were in Miraveda, I would've asked you to come and get me! Pleease! Let him go, he's not to blame! Pleeeaaase!"

Codrus, who did not look at her for a moment, said to Elaur through his teeth:

"Damn you bastard! I'll cut your throat like a chicken! Let me see how smart you are then! Anyway you've already got rid of me once!"

Then Elaur realized that the cold object at his throat was the blade of a knife and thought, terrified, that he could not get rid of Codrus's anger.

Anet, with tears in her eyes, continued to beg him:

"I beg you, Codrus! If you care about me, please forgive him! Please let him go home! I promise he will never upset you again!"

Codrus, who had not released his twisted hand or taken the knife blade from his throat, finally looked at Anet. Elaur immediately felt the grip of his hand weaken, and after a few moments, which passed painfully slowly, Codrus said to him, grunting:

"If Anet hadn't begged, I would've cut you like a chicken!"

He put his knife in a sheath hidden around his waist and pushed Elaur strongly in the direction they had come.

"Get the hell out of here! Come on, beat it until I change my mind! Beat it!"

Elaur, who had taken a few steps, avoiding the fall, still trembling and unable to believe that he was letting him go, quickly took his bag that had dropped on the ground and went back to school, wobbling, looking over his shoulder from time to time, in the darkness behind him. He turned left on the first street between the road and his street and ran like a madman, falling twice and arousing the dogs in the yards he was passing by.

When he was about forty yards from home, sweaty and still crazed with fear, he saw Gigi, Alena's boyfriend, who had just left them, barely recognizing him by the streetlight. When she got close to him, Elaur felt his feet trembling, he was unable to articulate any sound and he was breathing heavily. Gigi managed to grab him by the armpits, moved him on a bench to the right of the entrance gate, he picked up the bag that Elaur had dropped on the floor and put it next to him.

"Hey, what's wrong with you? What happened? Come on, calm down!"

Gigi, who was more than three years older than Alena and had just finished his military service, was also surprised by the horror that was still in Elaur's eyes:

"Come on! Try to calm down! Stay here and calm down until I take a bucket of water out of the well! If you drink a cup of water, you will recover immediately, he encouraged him."

The fountain, to the left of the gate, could also be used from the street, and Gigi turned really quickly the crank of the wooden drum, on which the chain was wound, at the end of which the metal bucket could be heard hitting the concrete pipes of the fountain. He grabbed the bucket of water, placed it on the edge of the well, and quickly filled with water an aluminum mug, which was fastened with a small chain to one of the pillars that supported the drum, and placed it next to the bucket. He walked the few steps that separated him from the bench, took Elaur by the armpits again and brought him slowly to the well, saying:

"Drink slowly until you finish the cup!"

He was still holding him, but he noticed that after a few sips, he wasn't trembling so much. He refilled the mug and said to him:

"You drink this too, just as slowly and then we sit on the couch and you tell me what scared you so much!"

He took him to the bench, then took off his jacket, which he put over Elaur's coat to protect him from the cold air and seeing that he had calmed down a little, he looked at him again, encouraging him with his eyes to speak:

"He waaan...teeed tooo k...kkkill me! He waann...teed toooo cut m...my throat!"

Two large tears rolled down his cheeks and seeing the confusion on Gigi's face, he continued:

"Codrus! He put the knife to my throat!"

He was breathing jerkily, while he dropped involuntarily two more tears! He stopped trembling and began to breathe almost normally.

Gigi knew what Codrus was capable of, but he didn't expect him to do such a thing to Alena's brother, who had nothing to do with the bullies from Miraveda. He arranged the jacket on his shoulders and said:

"It's a good thing your mother didn't see what you looked like. I was scared, let alone her! We stay here until you calm down completely and then I'll take you home! That way you can tell your people that you talked to me and that's why you were late! They had decided not to say anything to the family, and they would see what to do the next day."

He told his mother that he was not hungry because he had eaten at the pastry shop and went straight to his room, avoiding talking to anyone else. He wasn't able to sleep. Every time he fell asleep, he shuddered loudly, always seeing Codrus's knife, sparkling in the night.

Long after midnight, without turning on the light, so as not to attract his mother's attention, he took a book from the table and began to read under the duvet, by torchlight. He fell asleep late, when it was getting light. He was awakened at noon by Gigi himself, who had come especially to their house, during the lunch break, to bring Elaur the big news:

"Codrus has been arrested! You can relax now! He won't get out of there!"

Elaur wasn't good with such things, but he still didn't understand how Gigi had Codrus arrested.

"Well, I don't understand! How could he be arrested? So fast?"

"He stabbed Basamac's son at Strugurelu last night! He killed him on the spot!"

Chapter 14

Even though he had learned of the crime committed by Codrus, or perhaps that was why, it was beyond Elaur's capacity to go to school. Because neither he nor Gigi had told his family anything, he thought of telling his mother, when she came home from work, that he had been allowed to take some off days of school to prepare for a competition.

The news brought by Gigi, with the arrest of Codrus, not only did not reassure him, but made him relive the fear he had gone through, realizing, with horror, how determined he was to kill. He went back to bed and tried to resume reading the book he had read by torchlight, but the image of Codrus came back to him even stronger, making him read mechanically, without understanding anything, he would return over and over again at the beginning of the paragraph then losing the meaning of the text.

As he went out to the fountain, after taking out a bucket of cold water and drinking a cup, he heard some boys, four or five years younger than him, who had morning classes, playing football on the street. They had come from school and had already started playing football at two makeshift goals, one between their fence and the streetlight and the other between the fence of Lefan's yard and a stone placed as a bar. He saw from the sidelines his colleague's brother, Dode, three years older than them, who had just come from class, from the Economic High School and proposed him to get in the game, one for each team, but he said:

"Come on, man! Well, is this a real field? What could we play here?"

He had been refusing to play on the long, narrow "field" on their street for more than two years but he watched for a few minutes, probably remembering the terrific games from the years before, when he was the best. Elaur easily convinced the boys who were playing two against three, to let him get in the game, after they created new teams. He was with a younger boy in one team and the other three in the other team.

They played like that until dusk, running all the time between the two goals and constantly dribbling the opposing team, that was exactly what he needed to forget Codrus and the fear of the night before, at least for a while. He laughed after every successful dribble or goal, a forced, joyless laugh, confusing the four youngest children.

"Elaur, my boy, why are you home? You came earlier from school, Martia asked him, returning 'from the wallpaper', as she called her job, which was quite desirable in Miraveda and even in the City."

She had his rolled-up stencils under her arm and an old bag in her hand, in which she kept her brushes, the cotton twine and the vinyl ruler, as well as several open boxes of oxide, in all colors. Elaur, tired and sweaty, gazed at her and without answering the question, took her by the shoulders with his right hand, being about her height. He wanted to kiss her on the forehead but he kissed her left temple, as she slowly pulled her head.

"Wait, my boy, I'm dirty! I didn't even wash my face. I have wallpapered here, around the corner, at a neighbor's! I came quickly to boil some potatoes, to make you an oriental salad! I thought I had time to wash myself while the potatoes were boiling!"

Elaur was more than impressed with his mother's labor power, who had begun to earn quite well, but she worked 24/7, as she put it. During the day, she came home at least once or even twice, to quickly prepare food or do the laundry, as she tried to earn the much needed money, but also to organize the housework!

After washing well in a large basin with warm water from the stove, Elaur returned to the kitchen, where he ate a large plate of chicken soup, with vegetables and noodles, in which his mother would usually put three eggs instead of one. Then he went to his room and, as he was really tired, he fell asleep before the oriental salad was ready.

After midnight he woke up sweaty, having been chased by Codrus through a cornfield, where he had been picking up corn with the entire family the previous Sunday. All the other members of the family were gone and the corn rows, on which hung the white husks from which the cobs had been taken, seemed to be endless. After a few seconds of panic, opening his eyes, he recognized his room, dimly lit by the light bulb in the hallway of the house, the light of which penetrated sideways through the curtain at the top of the door.

Half asleep, wanting to go to the kitchen, he had put both feet on the jute rug with difficulty, trying to get up, but he fell back into bed, surprised that his legs refused to support him. He immediately remembered the crazy football he had been playing for over four hours, realizing that he had muscle soreness. He leaned down slightly, his chest above his knees, and began to gently massage his leg muscles. Trying to escape the nightmare, he thought of the words of old Mitu Urola, Dode's grandfather, a war veteran who was almost eighty years old: "Every event in a man's life is a lesson we must understand!"

He wondered what he should understand from the terrible incident he had gone through and from the crime committed by Codrus, failing to discern anything clear that would confirm the words of the wise old man. He had not known his grandparents, as both of them had died before he was born. So he had become attached to their neighbor, who was old and wise, with an almost hairless head, but with two white eyebrows, slightly wavy and unnaturally long.

Mitu Urola was also the street meteorologist and his predictions always came true. He always had something to tell, from his youth and especially from the three years he had spent in the war. He often drew general conclusions, which sounded more like education for the youngest.

He also began to massage his thighs, hitting them with the edges of his palms, at which point he remembered the remedy that a colleague on the school's football team had told him about, the water sweetened with sugar, drunk immediately after the effort. Although many hours had passed since the football was played on the street, he thought of drinking a cup of water, sweetened with two spoons of sugar, standing up with difficulty and heading for the winter kitchen.

He filled a cup from the habitual bucket of drinking water, in which he put the two teaspoons of sugar, mixing the sugar quite absent-mindedly, and sat down at the table covered with a white cloth with green flowers, and began to drink it in small sips, as a medicine.

Meanwhile, he saw a white bowl, and lifting the plate that was placed as a lid, he discovered his portion of oriental salad. He began to eat, just as absently, chewing almost mechanically, the pieces of boiled potato, dressed with vinegar and oil, along with the egg and onion slices, occasionally taking one of the small black olives mixed in the salad. In the end, after throwing the olive pips into the garbage can, he drank another half cup of water and, tormented by the muscle soreness, crawled into his bed, and fell asleep quite quickly.

The next day he woke up early and started to solve math problems, from the best and most famous collection, recommended by Mrs. Parvu. After about two hours, he took from his colleague, Dode, the homework for that day and solved it. He left for school with a lighter heart, twenty minutes before the school was going to start, walking slowly due to the muscle soreness. He did not want to talk to anyone about what had happened with Codrus, as he was still afraid of Butulan and even Basamac, the younger brother of the one who was killed. He just hoped he wasn't going to meet any of them.

In the first recess he was sitting thoughtfully in his bench, when Anet appeared in the doorway and signaled that she was waiting for him in the hall. He got up with difficulty and walked slowly to the window on the long upstairs hall, where she was waiting for him. With tears in her eyes and looking down, she slipped him a note and went to her class, avoiding to look at the others, so as not to notice her tears.

Elaur turned just as slowly to his bench, put the note in a notebook and seeing that no one was looking at him, picked it up carefully and read: “Please forgive me for what happened. I didn't know he was so crazy either. I beg you from the bottom of my heart not to tell anyone about it!” Five minutes later, Lefan, who was coming from the school yard, said to him:

“Have you heard about Codrus, that madman who beat us? He's under arrest! He killed Basamac, the brother of his friend!”

Elaur smiled bitterly and, thinking it was better to be ignorant, replied:

“He was a damn killer! He got where he needed to go!”

About two weeks had passed, during which time Miraveda was buzzing, after Codrus's murder. All sorts of rumors and suspicions appeared. Everybody told the story of what happened, but they also transmitted a lot of information, which was more or less fanciful. One of the statements, circulated by many people and attributed to the murderer's sister, came to Elaur's mind: “My brother was not like that, before that lawyer from the City hit him with the car five years ago!”

Life in Miraveda was slowly returning to normal, as was Elaur’s life, who was more concerned with the math recap, which he had imposed on himself, as he noticed that Peter was solving other problems in that collection than those for the eighth grade. After solving, out of curiosity, some fifth grade problems, and realizing that he had some shortcomings, probably due to the straight As he got easily, he decided to solve problems for a month for each of the previous three years, and then to deal with the eighth grade and the chapter with problems for the exams.

One day, during the last recess, seeing Lexia heading for the library, he also went there, all the more so as he waited for the return of a book he needed in the literature class, all six copies being borrowed by other students. As he entered, librarian Alicia, who liked him and had twice prepared him for the recitation contest, said rather bitterly:

"I watched specifically, but none of them was returned, although they have been borrowed for more than a month! I told everyone they weren't allowed to keep a book for more than two weeks, but in vain! I even went to the teachers' room and asked the teachers to force them to return the books faster, but nothing changed!"

Elaur thanked her and, pointing to the bookshelves, asked her:

"Can I take a look? I would like to get another book!"

As she agreed, Elaur walked to the corner opposite the entrance, where Lexia was waiting for him.

"I really wanted to look for you, she said, showing him a book by an English author. Are you free on Monday at seven PM?"

"I think so! At least so far I don't know if I have something to do! NYA meetings are always on Thursdays and anyway, they have not announced any."

"Are you interested in a debate about evolution and creationism?"

Elaur winced when he heard the topic of the debate, having a strange feeling that Lexia had the ability to read his mind.

"Not only does it interest me, but I really need it. I'll be there for sure at seven PM!"

He took the book proposed by Lexia, without studying it, as he was sure it was worth reading. Although he could not hear from a distance, it seemed to him that the librarian had been paying attention to what he had said to Lexia, so he went around the shelves a little and only then went to register the book in the file.

"Were you talking to someone back there or it just seemed to me?"

Elaur remembered Mrs. Vera's request to be discreet, and looking at Lexia, who had put a finger to her slightly pursed lips, he replied:

"I think I read something out loud! I can't speak English, but I really like how the English names sound!"

Miss Alicia, who was over forty years old, was quite confused by Elaur's explanation and, handing him the chosen book, looked once more at Lexia, moving her head in astonishment.

Elaur took the book, greeted it and went to his class. Next they had the literature class, with Professor Leacu, who reserved the last ten minutes to talk to them about his trip to Rome.

He spoke so vibrantly, happier than Elaur had ever seen him, showing them pictures of the Colosseum, Trajan's Column, and many other places in Rome. Looking at those pictures, Elaur had a strange feeling, as if he had lived in the days when the column was built. In his mind he had so many other images, which did not appear in Professor Leacu's pictures. At first they were very clear, then they were more difficult to discern, succeeding each other more and more quickly, more and more vaguely.

He felt dizzy, which made him almost fall off the bench and he recovered quite hard. He thought that those images could only be from a book he had read or at least browsed and he was glad that he had not fallen, so he avoided being embarrassed in front of his colleagues. The class was already over and Professor Leacu wanted to leave, after recovering his pictures of The Eternal City, when he heard Lefan:

"Are you going home, man, or do you want to sleep here?"

Elaur looked around in a state of bewilderment, quickly packed his things, and after stuffing them into the bag, went out with Lefan, recovering only after feeling the cold air of early December.

Chapter 15

It was two weeks before the winter break and less than three weeks before the Christmas holiday, but Elaur did not look forward to them with the same eagerness and joy of the previous years. Besides his torturous turmoil, the experience of meeting Codrus and the crime he had committed, had brought him a kind of forced maturity, accompanied by episodes of sadness, seemingly without cause, and nightmares, from which he had not yet escaped.

Martia noticed his mood swing quite quickly, but not knowing what had happened with Codrus, she hoped it was only a phase related to some whimsical girl. Elaur, in turn, knowing how much his mother loved him and how much she was affected by even his smallest problem, tried to make her understand that it was nothing important:

"I grew up too, mum! I want to be more serious!"

"I don't know what's in your soul and I know that you're not going to tell me either, but I noticed you're sad too often and I feel some kind of fear in your eyes! I don't what happened to you!"

"What fear, mum? How come you could see fear in my eyes? There is no fear and no sadness!"

"Hey, Elaur, my boy! When it comes to her baby, a mother is never wrong! Maybe it's bogus! God willing you're right and I worry in vain!"

She looked at him sadly, feeling that he was hiding something from her and she was not used to such a thing! She went to her bedroom and returned with a fifty-lei bill, saying:

"Look, go to a movie in the City, because it's Sunday! Don't bring me the change! You can also go to the confectioner's and you'll still have money for two or three books, because I know that you only think about that!"

Elaur kissed her on the forehead and remembered unwittingly a three or four-year-old event that had been imprinted on his mind when his mother had gone to their neighbor, Nion Urola, Dode's uncle, to pay a debt at the promised deadline. When she had borrowed the money, she had relied on a profit from her work, which had not come, and now she had to repay the loan, which meant almost the entire salary brought by Tramian. The neighbor in question, the eldest son of the old Mitu Urola, who had inherited a plot of land next to the old house, but also much of his wisdom, looked her in the eyes and asked:

"And then what's left for you? How can you live until the next salary?"

Martia looked at him thoughtfully and replied:

"On God's mercy! Let it be a lesson, not to count my chickens before they hatch!"

Her neighbor gave her back half of the sum and told her:

"You can't leave your children without food! Look, you can give these back to me in two installments, at the next salaries and don't worry as we won't starve!"

Martia, whose tears were already running down her cheeks, bent down to kiss his hand, but he took a step back and said:

"You don't have to kiss my hand, as if I were a priest! I know you are honest people! It's hard with three kids, but I know you're capable of moving the mountains for them! I help you as much as I can and I know that you will help yourself the best, as you are very skilled and hardworking."

Martia had left with tears in her eyes, but with the thought of what her neighbor had said. He was ten years older than her and she had great confidence in him. He never spoke without reason so she took into account his urging.

Now, as he knew how his mother managed to earn good money, it was Elaur's turn to understand what their neighbor, Nion Urola, had meant. He was the handyman who had taken care, without accepting any payment, of expanding their house a few years earlier, by adding two more bedrooms and a long hall.

Although it was the beginning of December, the weather was quite beautiful, with sunny days and rather spring temperatures. Elaur first went to the Flacăra cinema, which was located in the City center and he bought a ticket for the twelve o'clock movie, then he went down to the Great Park, where the Victoria cinema was, and bought a ticket there for the 4 PM movie.

Then he returned to the Center, where the Great Bookstore was, and after flipping through several books, he bought three of them from the "Books for All" collection and he had enough money left for the confectioner's. Between the two films, at the Pescăruș confectioner's, he asked for a cake, which a pretty lady, at his request, placed in a metal ice cream cup, adding two smaller cups of ice cream on top, one of cocoa and one of vanilla.

The next day, on Monday, after school, Elaur left just as hurriedly, taking the bag with him, to the Yellow House, where he knew that Lexia was waiting for him for a new debate. He had crossed the street in time and when he arrived, Lexia, dressed just as elegantly, was waiting for him right on the corner of the side street. They entered together through the same little gate and then through the oak door, which was open. In the hall on the ground floor were Mrs. Vera and another lady about the same age, both very soberly dressed.

"Good evening, ladies! Nice to see you again, Lexia said, bowing slightly."

Elaur also greeted, with the same condescension with which he greeted his teachers and headed to the spiral staircase. As he descended, he noticed that another row of four chairs had appeared, with only three empty seats left, including the chair he had sat during the first debate. He sat on that chair, noticing that the two twelfth-grade girls and the girl who was the same age as him were still there, the rest of them being high school students. Lexia had sat on the same couch at the end of the room, in line with the stairs and Professor Sofian and two others had already sat at the table on the stage.

After two more girls appeared, both of Elaur's age, occupying all sixteen seats in the hall, the two ladies came down and sat at the table.

“My name is Areta and I am a Latin teacher and Vera, my friend and colleague, double majored in philosophy and theology, miss Vivi is a biology teacher, Mr. Toma is a physics teacher, and Mr. Sofian is a philosophy teacher. The topic of tonight's debate is “Evolution vs creation and we will start from the idea that everyone present is familiar with the two theories, so we will move directly to the points of view in support of one theory or the other. Miss Vivi, please!”

The young biology teacher, after looking at those in the room, then at those that sat at the table, began her presentation:

“In order to be able to talk about the theory of evolutiona, we must first define the main characteristics of the living organisms, those that ensure the evolution of species, characteristics that are studied, scientifically proven and accepted even by most proponents of creation theory. First of all, we will define heredity as the ability of all living organisms to contain genetic information, on the basis of which morphological, physiological and behavioral traits are transmitted to the offspring. Their second characteristic is variability, which refers to random changes in individual traits in a population of organisms of the same species, also called genetic mutations, which, by accumulation, can produce radical changes in them, leading even to new species.”

Miss Vivi spoke quite clearly, but a slight tremble in her voice revealed her lack of oratorical experience. Encouraged by the two more experienced teachers, she continued:

"Finally, natural selection is the process by which individuals in a given population, who come to possess more effective characteristics for survival, will end up reproducing in much greater numbers than others, so that their descendants, who will inherit these characteristics, will represent the majority in the next generations. This is the very mechanism of evolution, a process that becomes stronger, from one generation to another, producing what we call adaptation to the environment and living conditions."

As she saw Professor Toma was eager to intervene, Mrs. Areta nodded.

"If we think about it, we are only apparently dealing with two different theories, regarding the emergence of life and especially of the human being. However, a theory arises through scientific methods, by applying logical arguments and especially experimentally proven, thus overcoming the stage of hypothesis. Exactly this scientific substantiation distinguishes the theory of evolution from the theory of creation, which is not even a theory, but an unverifiable hypothesis, based on Genesis and the existence of a divine plan, supported by faith and not by science."

Mrs. Areta, who had assumed the role of moderator, appointed her friend Vera to answer for Professor Toma. She said with the same warm voice that Elaur knew, but also with perfect calm:

"Professor, I listened very carefully to your speech, but I ask you, if you can explain to us, with such logical arguments and especially to test us, how do human thoughts arise and how do they turn into consciousness?"

Without waiting for the answer to the question, she continued:

"In fact, in His great wisdom, the Creator has conceived all beings to be perfectible and certain features of them, discovered only in the last centuries by science, are real and support a certain evolution, but not evolutionism. For this, you have to explain to us and especially to prove to us, the spontaneous appearance of the first life forms, but also the appearance of the human consciousness!"

Professor Toma, surprised by the gentle but head-on, counter-attack of Mrs. Vera and especially by the concreteness of her statements, replied:

"Regarding the appearance of the first life forms, all kinds of experiments are already being done, in environments that reproduce the Earth's atmosphere many millions of years ago, managing to separate certain amino acids, which are the basis of the appearance of life."

"It is easy to understand, Mrs. Vera replied, in the same warm voice, that many millions of years ago, no researcher lived, to determine scientifically how the Earth's atmosphere was, so those who reproduce the atmosphere of that time are based on what they think about it! In response to what you said a little earlier, I ask you now, how much is science and how much is faith in this experiment?"

"Mrs. Vera, you know quite well that certain phenomena and states can also be defined by logical induction, not only by laboratory measurements! To be understood by everyone, logical induction is based on the study of arguments, moving from a particular case that can be proven to a general case that indeed cannot be proven!"

Smiling discreetly, Mrs. Vera said, after looking warmly to the people in the room, interested in the reactions on the faces of those who were part of the audience:

"And this logical induction, by extrapolation on unverifiable situations, does not lead to unverifiable conclusions? I ask you then, what is the difference between such a conclusion and the creationist hypothesis, which you have also categorized as impossible to verify? I also ask you about the emergence of human consciousness, which clearly distinguishes us from any other known form of life, what environment do you think should be reproduced and what would be the scientific tools needed for such a test that is completely hazardous?"

Professor Toma, nicknamed Atom by his students, with a nice anagram, with the same teacher's tone, which came exclusively out of habit and not from disregard for the interlocutor, replied:

"Without such attempts, some of which are even risky, human knowledge would be almost completely blocked and we would return to the stage of the primitive man who, in the absence of scientific explanations for, say, the production of lightning, could only attribute them to supernatural forces!"

Mrs. Areta, more demanding and authoritarian than her friend, Vera, felt the need to get involved:

"It is by no means an obstruction of science, but an amendment of the exaggerated tendencies of hastily interpreting certain results, without the scientific rigor that you suggest in your first intervention. If the theory of evolution is based on science and the argument of proof, when this test is not performed, it would be desirable for certain hypotheses to be recognized as such and not presented as certainties, especially to a young and well-educated audience!"

Once again, Professor Toma was at least surprised by the logical rigor of the two ladies, from whom he expected, rather, certain dogmatic claims, easy to dismantle. Out of respect for this attitude, but also to conclude somehow having the upper hand, he proposed a small momentarily armistice:

"For certain things, which cannot be scientifically explained, it does not necessarily mean that such an explanation does not exist, but that it may not have been found yet!"

As in any armistice the conditions proposed by the other party must be taken into account, Mrs. Areta intervened, with the same exigency, but also with wisdom:

"I accept your assumption, provided you specify the nature of unproven hypotheses of these things, giving up relying on them as arguments! Mr. Sofian, do you have a point of view?"

"The debate is truly exciting and starting from the great gain of everyone's acceptance of the principle of the evolution of living organisms, all we have to do is go back to the two points of divergence, namely, the appearance of life and then of human consciousness! Your very arguments proved to me that we are not talking about two theories, but about two hypotheses, both equally beautiful and exciting."

Looking at everyone at the table, he continued:

"In this case, we could analyze, at least as a working hypothesis, the opinion of a friend of mine, an engineer, who is trying to reconcile the two hypotheses. He claims that more and more scientists are presenting the Big Bang, which would have led to the appearance of the universe, as an unimaginable explosion of a so-called 'singularity', a dimensionless quantity, but with an infinite energy and which, in his vision, can be an even more realistic description of the initial creation. He believes that this explosion entitles him to a certain 'quantum' definition of the Supreme Creator, as an infinite multitude of fragments of divinity, found everywhere and which, in the case of man, would even determine his consciousness!"

Mrs. Vera smiled, slightly intrigued, and Mrs. Areta, looking at her watch, said:

"Your hypothesis, or more precisely your friend's hypothesis, is as interesting as it is difficult to approach at this moment, seeming a modernist approach of the pantheistic conception!"

After a few moments of silence, Mrs. Areta also intervened:

"I think it is better to stop here, keeping it an open issue, as well as the possibility of those in front of us, to choose what suits them best, according to everyone's conscience and faith! First I want to thank Miss Lexia. You've been with us here thanks to her. Thank you too, good evening everyone and please remain discreet!"

After respectfully greeting everyone, Elaur said goodbye to Lexia, who had told him that she would be late with the two ladies and he was the first to leave the yard, then he headed home. He could see hundreds of large snowflakes flying in the dim light. It was the first snow of that winter. Satisfied with the debate, he tried to comply with Mrs Areta's invitation to choose what suited him best, eventually he was leaning towards Mr Sofian's hypothesis, which opened a new perspective for him to reconcile the faith in which he had been educated with all the knowledge he had gained at the school Miraveda.

When he got home, he ate with a big appetite a large plate of beans, with two large pickled red peppers and Martia noticed his bright face and bright eyes, so she thought that something had changed for the better for her son.

Chapter 16

The winter holidays, without snow and without the charm of previous years, had been as gray as the weather outside. The only moments when Elaur had left the book in her hand were during the evening visits of Gigi, Alena's friend, who was also quite passionate about reading. The only moments when Elaur left the book down were during the evening visits of Gigi, Alena's boyfriend, who was also quite passionate about reading. He was also the only one who noticed that his readings had nothing to do with the high school admission exam, as his mother thought. He had decided to take a break from preparing for the exam during the winter holidays, but his mother's belief was convenient for him, thus being relieved of her requests not to read at night, so as not to hurt his eyes.

He had given up reading only for two poker games and then for New Year's Eve, organized by the three Urola brothers at their house, a great opportunity for all seven boys present to fool around. Taking advantage of the absence of their parents, besides the traditional food, to which they had all contributed, on the table they also had some homemade sherry, three packs of Dunhill cigarettes, for which they had paid together, but also two new decks of playing cards, so New Year's Eve transformed, in fact, in a long night of poker.

Elaur had learned a little trick from Elu, as he noticed that he did not drink alcohol at all while playing poker. So, after they had all eaten, he sipped a little, only two or three times, from the sherry glass, more to avoid the ironies of the others, smoking all night, only two or three cigarettes. However, in the morning, besides a slight urge to vomit, he also had a diffuse headache. Considering that he and the two boys who remained in the game were winning, he announced:

"I'm leaving after this hand! My head hurts and I'm going straight home!"

After Lefan was the first to leave the game, Dode had vomited twice in the backyard and fallen asleep on a couch and now Elaur was "asking" to go home, Elu, tactfully counting his money, took the opportunity to make fun of them a little:

"That's it! This is what happens when you play poker with children!"

Elaur, who had almost doubled the amount he had started with, seeing that they were not upset, left immediately as he was bleary-eyed, and crossed the street to their house, where Alena with Gigi and four other couples from Miraveda were partying like crazy, dancing in the awning of the house, after the records with folk music, played on the family record player, with the volume turned up. He went straight to his room and fell asleep immediately, without being bothered in the slightest by the music, the groans and the cheers of the partygoers, which could be heard all over the house.

He woke up late in the evening, when his mother asked him to come to the "New Year's" dinner, to which she had also invited Gigi. His headache was gone and his urge to vomit was gone, but he didn't feel like eating so he took just a little Russian salad. After refusing the sherry glass, a fashionable drink in Miraveda, Gigi poured him a glass of ruby wine, thinking he had drank too much on New Year's Eve:

"You know the saying, fight fire with fire! Drink this glass and you'll recover!"

His completely wrong assumption attracted the attention of Martia, who was looking at Elaur in fright, praying in her mind to be like his father and not like her younger brothers, known for their heavy drinking!

After sipping a little wine, more to please Gigi, Elaur tasted some of the fried meat and pork sausage, which Martia would dress with two tablespoons of broth before removing from heat. Besides the pickle bowl, his mother had brought a smaller bowl full of sauerkraut juice, in which she had chopped two large onions, from which Elaur took one spoonful at a time, so he had to leave the table before everyone present finished eating.

Until the spring break, Lexia took him to two more interesting debates, which were also held at the Yellow House, in the same atmosphere of confrontation of ideas, but also of quasi-clandestine association. Elaur, with all his respect for the school, considered them more than welcome, the chosen subjects being suited for his worries, so as not to suspect Lexia that, by methods known only to her, she knew all his worries and anxieties. He read as many literature books, which had nothing to do with the school curriculum, to eventually attract his parents' attention. Martia even told him at one point:

"Elaure, my boy! With these books of yours, don't miss the exam! First you have to pass the exam, then you'll have the whole vacation to keep reading!"

He replied slightly annoyed:

"Is that how you know me, mother? Do you think I don't know what to do? I promise I'll pass the high school admission exam and still with good grades! I think Peter is the only one from Miraveda I can't beat! You will see!"

It was his way of making a promise, just to mobilize later, not to be laughed at.

"Know that I like your friendship with Peter! Isn't his father a psalm reader at the cathedral in the City?"

After Elaur nodded, she continued:

"His mother and I were good friends when we were young. I think he was born in May just like you, because we were pregnant at the same time and we were having arguments about who will give birth first!"

A week before the spring break, on Palm Sunday, together with Lefan and four other younger boys, they went to the willow and poplar forest on the southern edge of the city, to bring flowering willow twigs. According to tradition, these branches adorned the pillars of the gates and the windows of the houses, the most skilled of them made even small green-yellow arches, above the courtyard gates.

As the true winter had begun late, by the end of January, things changed in March, which had begun with a blizzard, and the cold that followed had delayed the beginning of the vegetation period for a long time, which was evident from the moment they entered the forest, the flowering willows being very few and with all the twigs at the base already picked.

After wandering through the woods, Elaur had set his eyes on a strange willow tree, which had, about two or three meters above the ground, a kind of green skirt, made of thick, tangled branches and above it, up to eight-nine meters high, only short, thin twigs, dried for a long time, so that only from up there to develop the most flowering and beautiful branches in the whole forest.

By the time Lefan arrived, he had struggled through the thick, tangled branches and began to check how strong the dry branches from above were. He had climbed, with great care, up to five meters, when he remembered the words of Tinu, his blind friend: "man's life can be like smoke. Now it is, but in the blink of an eye a gust of wind can destroy it!" He thought that it was much wiser to go down and be content with less flowering twigs, from the willow next to it, higher, but with green and very healthy branches.

"You're scared, aren't you? Let me climb and I'll have the most beautiful willow tree in Miraveda at the gate, Lefan told him."

"I think it's better to stay put! I tried those dry twigs and I don't think they are strong enough, especially since up there they are even thinner!"

Lefan, a daredevil as all boys his age, but more stubborn and fearless than most, holding between his teeth the knife with which he was to cut the flowering twigs, like the pirates seen on television, had gone through that tangle of branches and started to climb to the top of the willow.

After telling Lefan again to be careful, Elaur clung to a branch of the green willow beside him, he got up by the force of his arms and by a skillful movement, put his right foot and immediately the back of his left hand on the top of the branch, climbing it, like an exercise in physical education. He had deliberately inspired awe among the younger boys, to make them forget the test of courage which Lefan had won and in less than a minute he was at over twelve meters above the ground, one meter above Lefan. He took the knife he had received as a gift from Gigi out of his pocket, opened it and began to cut the willow twigs as well, throwing them down through the large branches of the tree.

He hadn't managed to cut more than twenty twigs, unlike Lefan, who had thrown more than thirty twigs to the younger boys on the ground, when he heard a short crack of broken wood and when he looked at Lefan, he saw him fall from more than eleven meters high. Trembling with fear, he instinctively looked at the branch he was holding and then, looking down, he saw Lefan lying motionless on the ground face up.

Terribly frightened, his hands shaking uncontrollably, he began to descend as fast as he could, terrified that Lefan had remained motionless. At the end of the descent, more and more panicked, he jumped directly from a branch more than three meters away, on the carpet of dried leaves at the base of the tree. The younger boys, unable to understand exactly the situation, after first laughing for a few seconds, as if at a successful joke, were now standing terrified around Lefan, not knowing what to do. Elaur quickly approached them, shouting desperately:

"Step aside! Step aside to let him breathe!"

He knelt and approached with his left ear to Lefan's mouth, to listen to him. He couldn't tell if he was breathing, because Stan, the youngest of the boys, who was only seven, started to cry, staring at Lefan.

"Stop this one, because I can't hear anything, Elaur shouted again, with tears in his eyes, scared by the white saliva that appeared in the corners of Lefan's mouth."

After they calmed him down, Elaur put his ear to Lefan's lips again and felt that he heard his breath. He looked up at the sky that could be seen among the branches of the trees, and after making another sign to ask for complete silence, he listened once more and shouted excitedly:

"He's alive, man! He's alive! I heard him breathing! I told him not to climb this damn willow!"

He listened to Lefan once more and convinced himself that he was breathing then, raising his head to where that twig had broken, he sighed deeply, trying to release all his tension. Then, more for himself than for the boys who looked at them, he said:

"He's alive! Thank God! What do I do now for him to recover? I'm afraid to move him, as we could hurt him even more! I would go to the City for help, but I'm afraid to leave him here, just with you!"

He looked in turn at Lefan and at Martac, the eldest of the other boys, who was in the fourth grade and from then on he was thinking of sending him to the first house at the edge of the forest, about a kilometer away, when Lefan moaned softly, but he didn't move, not even a little.

"Can you hear that? Can you hear?"

The boys nodded and Elaur, placing his right palm on Lefan's forehead, said:

"Lefan! Man, if you hear me, at least open your eyes a little! I beg you!"

He stared desperately at his motionless eyelids, blaming himself for not stopping him from climbing that tree, that stood like a death trap in their path. They knew each other from a young age, his mother was Martia's best friend and they considered themselves blood sisters until she died unexpectedly when they were in the first grade. He began to pat him lightly, alternately on both cheeks, as he had seen in the movies and after several sessions of patting, checking her breath, he said into his ear:

"Please! If you hear me, open your eyes a little!"

He looked at his eyelids in despair, as the other boys did, but after a few moments he thought that perhaps his eyelids would be harder to move for him and he said:

"Come on, boy! Please! Move something! If you can't move your eyelids, move at least one finger! Please!"

All eyes had shifted to Lefan's fingers as he moved slowly two fingers from his right hand. Elaur looked at the boys, as if he was afraid it had been just his imagination and when he saw their happy faces, he sprang to his feet and didn't know what else to do.

"He's alive! Crazy Lefan is alive! If he recovers, you'll stay here with him and I'll run to the hospital to call for help!"

He flinched when he thought he heard a "no," coming from Lefan and leaned over him immediately and asked:

"Am I dreaming or did you say 'no'?"

Lefan moved his eyelids a little and he said very slowly, without opening his eyes:

"Stay...! Stay... here!"

Elaur cried with joy, then the others began to jump up for a few moments, until he motioned for them to stop, addressing Lefan again:

"Think well! Maybe it's better to call an ambulance! Look, I'm sending Martac!"

"No… I don't want… amm… bulance…"

Elaur thought for a moment, confused by his friend's refusal, and asked:

"How do you feel? Where does it hurt the worst?"

"My back! Stay here, I'll be alright!"

After more than half an hour, as he talked to Elaur, he got much better and he whispered looking up:

"If it weren't for these lower branches, I'd be dead! These slowed me down!"

They stayed with Lefan for almost another hour and spent the same time on the road. They arrived in Miraveda with five or six branches each, but also with Lefan's indication, not to talk to anyone about the accident.

On the second day of Easter, when the generous spring sun caressed all living things, he remembered his blind friend, whom he had not seen for so many months. He thought he might be on the high bank, enjoying the weather, so that he would be comforted by the sun's rays too. He took a book and the blanket and went to the valley, where he hoped with all his heart to see Tinu again.

As soon as he reached the end of the street, near the plot, he saw his unmistakable figure, sitting in the same crouching position, as if he were looking far away, towards the edge of the universe. In two minutes he arrived near him, greeted him, and said:

"I'm so glad to see you again! I didn't know anything about you anymore! How are you?"

Tinu smiled enigmatically, turned his head to Elaur and replied knowingly:

"I'm also glad to hear you, Elaur! I'm fine, I don't have much to do, except to pay attention to the world around and the few people I can talk to! It's nicer here than in the Capital, in my studio apartment, but I don't really have anyone to talk to!"

The ground was still cold and Elaur spread his blanket and, sitting down, invited Tinu to move on the blanket next to him. Then he told him the story from the Palm Sunday and he acknowledged that his very warning had saved him from a tragedy. He told him about his friend Lefan, the scare he had experienced and the remorse that he had not been able to stop him. He even told him about his mother, who had died seven years earlier after a failed, secret abortion.

"Give me your hand to see what's wrong with you! I feel you are very tense."

Elaur held out his hand and without Tinu asking, he put his other hand on his heart. After a while, he said to him:

"Your friend was protected by his mother! God forgave her, just to take care of her son, whom she left so young. But you've also gone through extreme difficulties. Someone threatened your life!"

Surprised, even frightened, Elaur muttered a tormented "yes", but Tinu continued unperturbed:

"There was a girl there too! Don't be mad at her! She doesn't know, but you have to know! He was there to save you, not to endanger you! Your meeting with that man could not wait and that's the only way you could move on, but you don't have to be afraid any more! His anger will leave as it came!"

They sat together for a long time, without him reading any line from the book he had with him, but in which Tinu told him about the Braille alphabet, about the school he went in the Capital, where he had passed the seven classes, as they were supposed back then, with the help of that alphabet, but also with noble teachers, who struggled to explain many things to them, which were hard to understand as his eyes had never seen anything. He had also attended a vocational school, where he had learned to do therapeutic massage and worked at a hospital until a year ago, when he retired earlier than those without physical disabilities.

He went home, delighted by such a friendship, thinking of what he had said about Anet, whom he had judged very harshly.

Chapter 17

In Miraveda, which had not even passed a hundred years of existence, a collective mind had already been created and the opinions of the majority became almost rules, even gaining proverbial value. Most of the inhabitants of the former commune, to which were added the "foreigners", as those from the nearby communes were called, who bought or built houses in Miraveda, had little or no schooling. Accustomed from an early age to working the land, they longed for the easier, or at least better paid, work of the few existing craftsmen. The adage, "A handful of trade is a handful of gold" may not have been invented in Miraveda, but here it was absolute sovereign.

Most of the parents, who had difficulty supporting their children during the eight compulsory years of schooling, after those eight years, they were sending them to the two-year vocational schools, but they urged them especially to become apprentices, as they needed only six months of schooling. They could not even be accused, as long as most of the children were also attracted by the short period of schooling, by the granted scholarships, but also by a safe job, immediately after graduation.

Thus it was not surprising that from his class only eight students out of thirty opted for high school, with only one girl among the eight. In the other three classes there were even fewer, in total, about eight or nine students. Unfortunately Elaur would never see again most of those who chose the apprenticeship set up next to the big factories in the Capital, some kind of huge ogres who swallowed thousands of children from the province.

Only one girl, beautiful and very neat, but who had gained weight in recent months, surprised everyone, declaring in the last two weeks that she would not continue at any school, although she had quite good marks. In the last three days of school, after seeing she had got all her marks, she did not even come to school. Elaur found out from his sister that she had already married a bulldozer operator who was renting a room in her parents' house. A week earlier, he had evicted his wife and two children back to the village they had come from seven years earlier to escape poverty and working the land.

After another two weeks, the girl's parents, who had not yet turned fifteen, sold the house in Miraveda and moved with her and their new son-in-law to a smaller town about forty kilometers down the The Great River. It was only after a year that the meaning of the story was found, which had surprised and saddened Elaur, when his former colleague appeared in the teachers' room of the school in Miraveda, to pick up his graduation certificate, with her six-month-old child in her arms. At that time was applied a custom known by everyone, before the law. When a minor became pregnant with an adult man, he had to choose between two options, marriage or imprisonment.

At the end of the eight years of schooling, Elaur thought that it was no longer necessary to appear at the awards ceremony, which was held on the same stage that was also an open-air cinema. If in previous years he was looking forward to the graduation ceremony, now it seemed childish to go on stage to receive his diploma.

Before the awards announcement, there was quite a long show organized by the students of the school, but to which the recent graduates no longer contributed, as they were busy with the preparation for the admission exams. The stage, located in the courtyard between the church and the dispensary, was a rather imposing concrete construction, one meter high and quite spacious, with a high and slightly arched wall in the back, also used as a screen.

At the big "ceremony" almost the entire village gathered to accompany the students and enjoy their show. After the ceremony, parents and children left for their homes, some were happy, others were upset and some were satisfied that "the little one passed the grade". However, no one dared to question the teachers' objectivity or the awards.

That afternoon, Elaur was reading relaxed from the history textbook, when his younger sister, who had also finished second grade, came, slightly puzzled, and announced him that a teacher was waiting for him in the room by the street, which in Miraveda was the guest room. As he entered the room and saw his mother with tears in her eyes, Elaur looked in astonishment at Mrs. Stara, his headmistress, who had a big smile on her face, however:

"Well, Elaur, why did you miss the award ceremony right now, when you've been top of your class? Now that I brought you the diploma and carried your books home you have to pay me!"

He was sincerely glad to see the books on the table, but reading the grade on the diploma, the same as the one he had calculated, which he thought was smaller than Arian's, he looked up in astonishment at his former headmistress:

"I put you both in first place, but Arian has a grade five hundredths lower than yours!"

Elaur, looked once more at the six books on the table, smiled a little confused, not knowing what to say, while Martia, happier than ever, went to the kitchen, and returned with a big glass of cold water, in which she had put a teaspoon of pink roses sherbet, which she placed in front of the headmistress. Mrs. Stara, who was a gentle woman close to her students, a biology teacher, but who also taught agriculture at the school in Miraveda, a subject taught in schools from the country, said:

"Thank you for the treatment, but I think Elaur and even you deserve more than me this sherbet!"

Martia apologized and left immediately, then she brought another tray, two more glasses of water with a teaspoon of sherbet in them and placed them on the table. Intimidated by the headmistress's special attention, Elaur stared at the blue vase with three plastic roses, which was put on the doily in the middle of the table, knitted by Martia from macrame. Encouraged by the teacher, he began to eat the sweet and fragrant sherbet. He also sipped the water, while his mother, listening to Mrs. Stara praise her boy, was all smiles and completely forgot about the sherbet in front of her.

Shortly afterwards, he had the admission exam, at which, after both written tests in literature and mathematics, Elaur went home in silence, satisfied only with half of what he had done. He was a little afraid of the multitude of students that went out after each test in the high school's inner courtyard and of the relaxed attitude many of them displayed. The tests had not been easy at all and he felt he had a pit in his stomach, as he was thinking about the announced competition of over three candidates for one place. He was afraid that he would be overrun by many of the candidates, as most of them came from schools in the city. He had agreed with his family not to accompany him or to discuss the exams, except after the oral tests, at which the marks were communicated immediately.

He recovered only after the oral literature exam, to which he had drawn a generous test, which consisted in describing a character from a well-known play. He had become the surprising winner of a messy political competition, in which two other politicians had been favorites, after blackmailing the right person with a compromising love letter, accidentally lost. He had read by chance in a memory book how, before completing the work, the friends of the brilliant author, acquainted with what he had written, bet sometimes on one or the other of the two favorite politicians. Both of them were villains, but quite different. The first "excelled" in stupidity and the second in demagoguery. So they were both qualified, from a satirical point of view, to win. To everyone's surprise and amusement, the author had conceived a third character, who suddenly entered the election race and won, with the justification that "he is dumber than the first and more demagogue than the second".

He had begun the presentation with this evocation, watching with delight how the faces of the three members of the committee had lit up at the same time, so that after another three or four sentences the chair of the committee would stop him and congratulate him. He got an A, which gave him wings and made him run home to bring the good news to his mother.

The next day, in mathematics, the subject seemed to him quite easy, though very laborious, but as he had had time to make sure that he had not erred in his calculations, after writing the solution on the board, he came out happy, with a second A.

He drew a rather difficult subject at the history test, perhaps because it was approached quite superficially in the eighth grade textbook. After two or three sentences, when the members of the commission saw, in the examination sheet, the two As, one of them stopped him and asked him a rather simple question and after answering, after he had consulted the other two, he informed him that he also got an A. Quite surprised by the ease with which the third A had come, he could not help thinking that he had escaped the stress of the admission. He left for home just as quickly and in a rather serious voice said to his mother:

"Mom, you should see what happened! There's been a misunderstanding! I don't have two As at the exam!"

He paused for a moment, to watch her reaction, but also the reaction of his father, who joined her and looked at him puzzled.

"I don't have two As because... I have three As!"

Martia slapped him lightly on the scalp, which sounded more like caress and she said very happily:

"Ugh, you scared me, you scoundrel! You resemble only your father with these unbearable jokes."

Then she hugged him, kissed him on both cheeks and said to Tramian:

"Tell me, my husband, how much money do you give the boy for bringing you three As?"

Tramian, who was trying to hide his excitement, immediately changed his expression and said:

"You should give him money, my wife! Because you two chose high school!"

Martia felt that much of her husband's anger had melted away like a charm, she entered the house, from where she returned with two hundred lei bills and offered them to Elaur, saying:

"I don't have more, as I would have given you all the money! And you, Tramian, all you have to do is be proud of your boy! For free!"

When the final results were displayed, the ninth place on the list of the admitted exceeded any expectation for Elaur, but that year's bombshell was the first place winner, none other than his friend Peter. As Arian was also admitted, on the fifteenth place, another boy from the eighth D class was on the nineteenth place and his neighbor Dode, on the twenty-third place, the results of the admission quickly became a good source of pride for the modest and rural Miraveda.

The surprises were not over because Elaur noticed right next to their small group two of the boys from the City, who had impressed him in the previous days as they were walking through the high school yard with confidence. Now they were looking lividly at their dressed up parents, who did not understand how their boys, "so well prepared", could not be admitted.

Unwillingly, he saw himself playing poker, bluffing, but immediately dismissed the mischievous thought, looking to another boy from a commune west of Miraveda, who was looking at him extremely cheerfully, happy with the result.

He had joined their group from day one, after the written math test. He validated his results of the solved problems, with him but especially with Peter and befriended both of them! Among so many arrogant figures, he had caught his attention with his very friendly manner and the ever present smile on his face, seeming as intimidated as him by the exam, but especially by that crowd of students.

Contrary to expectations, although he was happy for such a good result, he was a little intimidated by the new world he had just plunged into, more complicated and more challenging than his simple and wonderful Miraveda. As he arrived home, the immeasurable delight of his parents made him forget any worries or intimidation. To the general joy was added his gratitude that he had made his parents so proud and happy.

Almost two months of vacation followed, in which his friendship with Lefan, who had enrolled in the Vocational School for Chemists, already gave him a sense of nostalgia, feeling that their paths would slowly part. He went almost daily with him, but also with Dode and other younger boys, fishing on the Grand Canal, on the Youth beach, the name of a wild beach, located on the same left bank as the City, but located two kilometers from it and about four from Miraveda.

Elaur couldn't swim and at that beach the depth of the water suited him, which increased progressively. It also didn't have the dreaded pits in which the reckless, but even experienced swimmers lost their lives, year after year. The water was quite clean and the sand was very fine, but they had to bring drinking water and sometimes even food from home, unlike the beach on the other side, opposite the Great City Park, where there was a kiosk with sweets, juice and even beer, but also a football field, with wooden goals, a volleyball court with a net, as well as rings and a fixed bar, for strength exercises.

He loved that wild beach, where he felt at ease with the simple boys from Miraveda, playing games known or invented by them, having more fun than ever. They learned together how to make some kind of sundial, by drawing a circle on the sand and placing a stick in its center. The whole secret was the position in which the line for twelve o'clock was placed on the circle, and diametrically opposite, they drew the line for six o'clock. In the middle of the two equal arcs, they then put three o'clock on the right and nine o'clock on the left, finally completing the signs for the other hours. A passenger boat commuting between the City and a commune in the neighboring county, located on the other side of the river, who was passing at the same time, had helped them to position, better and better, the line for twelve o'clock, so that the shadow of the thin stick in the center of the circle indicated the time with fairly good accuracy. He wanted to enjoy his group of friends in Miraveda as much as possible, as a small world from which he would somehow part, feeling that many things would change in his life. In the few minutes spent in front of the admission list, he had seen many boys with whom he could become friends, but also several smart and sophisticated girls, who intimidated him but also provoked him, in a way he had never felt before.

But he could not be completely satisfied with that summer without working at least a week at the Farm, as much as to satisfy his ambition to earn his own money, feeling that you can't respect enough the money received from your parents if you don't know how hard it is to earn it yourself.

Instead of a week, they spent ten days as farmhand in the sunflower field, a prolongation which was due to a former colleague from the eighth C class and future high school classmate, Ariana, a blonde girl with blue eyes, to whom he was attracted, especially since he had entered a competition with an older boy, who also liked her and who did his best to work only next to her.

He had learned to sharpen his own hoe every night by hammering it on an anvil and he obtained a better edge by flattening it. Gigi, who was going to marry Alena and who came to them more and more often, was the one who showed her how to do it, but he also warned her one evening:

"You sharpened it enough! See how you use it tomorrow! Watch your feet, don't give it meat!"

He listened to what his brother-in-law said, though he was displeased by the expression he used, and acknowledged that, two or three times, it was not long before he stuck its sharp edge in his foot, as he was looking at Ariana.

After ten days he decided not to go to the farm, as his attraction to Ariana faded as quickly as it had appeared.

Chapter 18

The first year of high school, in which the school curriculum was the same for all seven classes, had further strengthened Elaur's determination to choose, from the second year, the humanities, despite the fact that all his friends in Miraveda had focused on science from the beginning.

Among the boys from Miraveda, he had been in the same class as Peter and Vior, a boy who lived on the road on the opposite side of the mill at the entrance in Miraveda, but who had finished middle school at the number one school, which was the best in town. He had soon become his best friend.

His very calm manner, very discreet expression and patience to listen to others, made him the ideal friend for the temperamental and talkative Elaur so they felt very good together. Vior responded to his frothy and captivating speech with a very laconic style, almost mathematical, but mutual empathy brought them closer, their conceptions and concerns were quite similar and further strengthened their friendship.

Mrs. Culia, their teacher, had quickly become Elaur's perfect role model for the high school teacher. More demanding than any of the teachers at the school in Miraveda, she had impressed him with her almost perfect command of the German language, which she taught in their class, but also with her knowledge of three other international languages. The daughter of a psalm reader at a church in the city, married to a well-known lawyer, poet and amateur archaeologist, at the age of forty-five, was dignified with her impeccable attire and demanded the same from her students, being equally loved and feared by them.

Beyond the German classes, which had made him love this language, so different from the Romance languages, she was an exceptional headmistress who followed closely the evolution of her students, from the school situation to their attire, as she talked to them about the value of etiquette and good manners, but also about fairness, verticality and last but not least, about humanism. In her more than twenty years of teaching, she got used that not all students resonated with her efforts, but she did not despair because of that and she was ready to do the same things, even if only one student was receptive to her advice.

After the first trimester the literature teacher went on maternity leave, and Mrs. Culia, after taking over her classes, became the most important teacher in high school for Elaur, as she represented not only the standard of seriousness and fairness, but also of a surprising, though carefully censored, human warmth. In his turn, although he did very well in German classes and had excelled in supervision classes, he made a very good impression on Mrs. Culia only in the middle of the second trimester, in literature classes. He had worked for many hours, in the two weeks they had, on the first synthesis paper, on the comparison between classicism and romanticism, a work of over twenty pages, secretly hoping that he would be the one nominated to read it in class. Really surprised by the quality of the work, but especially by the very consistent documentation, she asked him thoughtfully:

"Elaur, what section do you want to choose in the second year?"

"I am determined, since middle school, to study humanities!"

Mrs. Culia smiled knowingly and said:

"It means we will work together until the end of high school. I hope the joy is mutual!"

Elaur was more pleased with this remark of the headmistress than with the A he had got, even though it was the first A in literature since the beginning of high school.

However, he was the most delighted with his special relationship with the young and beautiful teacher Roza, the French teacher, whom he had enchanted with compositions made in Voltaire's language. As it was her first year of teaching, Miss Roza had managed to ignite many secret passions, especially in the minds of the students, but even of some of the teachers, even though most of them were married.She had finished college with very good grades and showed not only pedagogical talent, but also an extraordinary exigency, which had cut off the momentum of some of Elaur's colleagues, whose secret libido had dropped dramatically after an F.

Their revenge was to put all the pieces of chalk on the top frame of the board, where Miss Roza reached only by stretching very hard, lifting her miniskirt quite a lot, to the exaltation of all the boys. Until she understood what was at stake with this little monkey business, determined to solve this challenge, she took the necessary chalk on her own.

Only after three or four such incidents, before going to the blackboard, smiling mysteriously at the big lugs in the last rows, did she take out of her elegant purse a small bag in which she had two whole pieces of chalk.

Miss Roza, born and raised in a good family of intellectuals from the Capital, although she did not exceed one meter sixty-five centimeters, had a very beautiful body, highlighted by tight dresses and miniskirts, but also very beautiful features, blue eyes and dark hair, with a French haircut and carefully arranged. In addition, she had a special distinction with which, combined with a perfect calm and the smile of a true Mona Lisa, she managed to confuse men instantly, as she tamed even the deputy director, nicknamed the "sheriff," for the harsh physical corrections applied to the students, but who, in the face of Miss Roza, looked like a troubled teenager.

When writing frequent compositions in French, with topics chosen by their beautiful teacher, his passion for literature, plus the appropriate dictionary, which he had to borrow each time from his neighbor Dode, helped him to compete with success against Geta, who knew French better than everyone in the class.

In the first quarter, with a B and two As, plus an A in the final thesis, he had the highest grades in French, tied with Geta. At the beginning of the second trimester, for a composition for home, in which, for more than an hour, he could not write a single sentence, so he decided to tell Miss Roza frankly, right at the beginning of the class, that he had no inspiration and could not do his homework, relying on her sympathy for him.

As he was delighted, however, by Mrs. Culia's request to go to another class that spoke German like them, to exemplify the difference in pronunciation of the letter "h" in the words *ich* and *noch*, especially since there were some pretty girls in that class, he was five minutes late. When he entered the classroom, Miss Roza, with the grade book in her hand, checked the homework notebooks, already putting three Fs. When she reached him, after four more Fs, Elaur solemnly declared:

"I did not understand the topic of the composition at all and I could not write anything. You know how much I like compositions, but I struggled for over an hour and I couldn't write anything. I don't think it's fair to be punished!"

Looking at him candidly, Miss Roza said to him:

"I'm sorry for you, you write very good compositions, but it is unethical for your colleagues not to receive the same grade as them."

At the next lesson, although he had the homework notebook in front of him, in which he had solved the exercise he had received for home, at the beginning of the class, he stood up, looking angrily at his precious Miss Roza and made a second solemn announcement:

"As a sign of protest, for the F you gave me last time, I did not do my homework for today!"

Miss Roza, looking at him in surprise, opened the grade book and said to him, calmly:

"I am sorry for you but you get an F!"

Elaur, who had meanwhile sat down, stood up, proud of his decision, and said to her:

"I don't understand why you give me an F!"

"Because you didn't do your homework!"

"In that case, why don't you give me an F minus?"

"Isn't F minus a grade for those who don't do their homework?"

"That's up to me, not you!"

"Please, at the end of the next break, show up at the teachers' room!"

At the end of the break, after entering the teachers' room, he was sent by the deputy director to wait in the hall, not before glaring at him, under his long, thick eyebrows, which more terrible than two ears of oats, over which the frost had fallen, a sign that the sheriff was aware of the "crime" he had committed, for which he would be held accountable.

He had been received in the teachers' room, after all the teachers had left, and only the seraphic presence of Miss Roza prevented Elaur from getting a "spade" from the Sheriff, as the students called his terrible slap, with which he had become feared among students. After muttering a few words as explanations and being asked to apologize, Elaur went to his class, somehow upset that he had not received that slap, to see how much Miss Roza could endure for his principles, but especially for herself.

With all his attention to literature and languages, Elaur finished the first year with very good grades in mathematics and physics, being lucky enough to have two very good teachers. At least in mathematics, Professor Petronius, who was none other than the husband of his first teacher, Mrs. Dida, from the school in Miraveda, had a method very similar to the style of his middle school teacher, Mrs. Parvu, who was beneficial for the best students who showed quick thinking. After each lesson, he would write a problem on the blackboard, from the newly taught subject, and whoever solved it first would go to the blackboard and explain it. For two or three such problems solved, you received an A in the grade book. Elaur and five or six of his colleagues received almost all the grades.

If in high school Elaur almost never studied at home, this lightness was no longer possible in high school. In many subjects, but especially in geography, geology and even Latin, where he had very demanding teachers, he had to repeat the lesson several times to get a reasonable grade. He had finished the first year with a pretty good gpa, being surpassed only by Peter and the hard-working and ambitious Geta, who, like him, had also opted for the humanities. They would be colleagues, with the same headmistress and literature teacher, Mrs. Culia.

In the last week of the school year, Mrs. Culia had even taken three of his classmates to the blackboard, who had already failed other subjects and if one had failed other subject besides German literature or language, he would become a repeater who must pass the admission exam again. After writing down the grades on a piece of paper and not in the grade book as before, she called Elaur to the foreign language office to help her finish the school records, a task that proved to be quite delicate.

"Oh, Elaur, this scoundrel of Oltea, if I don't give him a C in the third trimester, then he's a repeater and puts his poor mother in the grave, who already has a troubled heart! This week he did well, because he's not stupid, but what grade should I give him, as he has two Fs and a C for his final thesis? I'd give him a B minus, is that enough?"

"That's not enough, madam! Not even a B is enough! He will pass only with an A!"

"Heaven forbid! How can I give this bastard an A? But please, spare me your mental calculations! Calculate with the pencil on paper! Maybe a B is enough because I am not giving him an A even if you cut my hand!"

"Believe me, madam! It's not enough! But there is another very simple solution!"

"Don't make me change a grade in the book, because I'll never do such crap!"

"No, madam! He'll pass if you give him two B minus in two different days!"

With her face suddenly lit up, Mrs. Culia said to him:

"I knew you were a smart boy! I know four foreign languages in vain, as only mathematics is the "foreign language" for me!"

She made him do the calculation on paper, too, to be sure, after which, smiling bitterly, she said:

"What am I supposed to do, Elaur? I'm also thinking of their parents! They spend the money with them, and the scoundrels don't study, at least enough to pass! Let's fix the situation for the other two, because I see you're good at it! These fools should buy you a drink or a present, because without you, I wouldn't know how to save them!"

In the end, Elaur thought that he had earned much more than the gift of his colleagues, as he had learned the lesson from Mrs. Culia. It was a lesson about exigency and humanism.

Chapter 19

During the first year of high school, in addition to the books included in the curriculum, Elaur's time for reading had decreased more than he had thought, as the demands of teachers, from the nine subjects of study, were completely different from those in middle school. The laborious homework, the lessons from geology, geography but also others, which could not be easily retained, but also the generous attention allocated to the compositions from French literature and language, occupied him most of the time.

He had gladly discovered that the high school librarian was his mother's cousin, but this had helped him more to borrow the books he needed for literature lessons than to borrow other books. The summer vacation, however, had come as a blessing, from this point of view. On the last day of school, after he chose six books from the library and continued to search through the cramped shelves, the librarian said to him:

"That's enough for a month! When I come back from vacation you can come and get some more! How is Martia? I haven't seen her in years!"

"She's working! Now it's her busy season. She works from five in the morning until eight or nine in the evening."

"Oh my God! Is that so? Please tell her to slow down, so she doesn't get sick!"

On the way home, Elaur thought only of what his aunt had said, and as he was of the same opinion, he decided to have a serious conversation with her that very evening. Martia arrived home shortly after nine o'clock. In her bag of paints, she had added a two-hundred-watt light bulb to work in the early morning or evening, when she didn't have enough light, so she managed to put wallpaper on two or even three rooms a day. Worse, for a few days, even though it was mid-June, she coughed badly and had a fever.

"Mom, why don't you stay home for two or three days until you get well?"

Martia, looking at him gently, replied:

"You know your stuff, I know mine, my boy! If I stay home a single day, I turn all my appointments upside down, let alone two or three days. And then if I stay home, the money doesn't come if I do nothing!"

"I thought more than you think about this wallpaper work. You work about fourteen to fifteen hours a day. As you have so many customers, if you increase the price, at least as much as your work is worth, you can earn the same money, working ten hours a day and not destroying your health!"

"Hey, my boy! God gave me this job so I can raise you! The women from Miraveda earn a quarter of my money at the Farm and they work all day long in the sun! I, in addition to how much I earn, for better or worse, I also go home and cook something for you or wash some clothes, so you have something to wear!"

"Mom, the women at the farm work half the time you work and they haven't bothered to learn your trade. On the other hand, if this job is so in demand, then it has to be paid for! Even if you lose a few customers, you will earn the same money, but working in humane conditions!"

"I don't complain about clients, my boy, but if I get greedy, God takes what he gave me. I ask as much as I value my work! Greed spoils the people!"

Although she did not really agree with what her mother said, Elaur loved and respected her for the way she treated others, for which she was loved and respected by everyone in Miraveda. He could ask his mother anything, but not give up her principles, which not only enable her having good relations with everyone, but also gave her a great spiritual satisfaction. Seeing that her son was thinking, Martia continued:

"When you get to sell your soul for money, you have come out of God's hands, and the devil is waiting!"

He gave up, but his mother's words settled quietly in his head, haunted him his entire life and were deafening in his mind whenever he was tempted to give in to greed or the ease of judging the work of others.

He divided the first month of his vacation between the Youth beach and his love of reading, which, as it extended into the night, had turned his friend Lefan into a kind of alarm clock, as he almost never managed to go to the beach before ten o'clock, walking an hour on the road.

Also on vacation, at first only on Sundays, but then on other days, he started walking in the evening to the City Center, but also on the alleys of the Central Park, with his new friend, the quiet and friendly Vior. He did not take

Lefan's place, but rather his stepbrother's place, Nic, with whom he had had many interesting discussions about friendship, life, and even love in recent years. Quite often, the discussions with Nic, three years older than him, were quite exciting and helped Elaur to polish his phrasing technique, but also the rigor of logical argumentation. Nic, who wasn't worse than the boys who had gone to high school, had chosen and finished, for financial reasons, the vocational school of chemical operators, which Lefan now attended. After finishing school, he was employed at the factory that owned the school, but he had also entered high school, at the evening classes, practically he was busy all day.

Elaur already lacked the interesting discussions with him, seeking in the meetings with his new friend, the charm of these real debates. Unlike Nic, he was excited extremely rarely but Vior was still an equally good partner for discussion. His short, but interesting and objective interventions were sufficient for new and challenging developments of the subject in question. As they were complementary, the two friends got along almost naturally, spending more and more time together. Vior appreciated Elaur's verve and creativity, and he found the perfect interlocutor, who understood his ideas, sometimes completed him, but especially, endured his captivating style and carefully followed the numerous parenthetically pauses on the edge or in the continuation of the initial discussion.

Despite all the temptations and pleasures of the holidays, Elaur did not go beyond his ambition to work for ten or fifteen days. This time he found a more enjoyable activity at a vegetable farm than the work in the field and he was also paid better. In the shade of a warehouse that had only a roof, sitting comfortably on an inverted crate, they broke the bell peppers brought in large crates from the field, in four or five pieces, removing their tails and seeds and placing them in smaller crates, which at the end of the day they set off for a cannery, forty miles from the city.

At that farm, located beyond the commune bordering the City, on the opposite side of Miraveda, the payment was not made for the working day, but for the number of boxes filled with broken peppers. This suited Elaur, because in the end he won well, but he also stood out in terms of jokes and jokes, which turned every day of work into a kind of pleasant get-together. Unfortunately, after about ten days, the activity was greatly reduced. Only the women who had been there since spring remained at work.

As only half of the holiday had passed, Navy Day was a good opportunity for Elaur and the boys from Miraveda to go to the Great Park, to watch the festivities and the funny competitions, organized on this occasion. Navy Day, with a tradition of over seventy years, celebrated from the beginning on August 15, the religious feast of St. Mary, the patron saint of sailors throughout the Christian world, had been moved by the New Authority, for ideological reasons, on the first Sunday in August, and any religious connotations were removed.

In front of the Great Park, whose main alley also served as a seafront, about fifty yards from the shore, had been anchored the captain's ship, on which were several officers, dressed in suits and ties, sweating heavily next to a paunchy Neptune, with a red cloak and a trident in his hand, who had nothing to do with the tradition of the people of the river, but still made the children present happy.

After a boring and poorly released speech, the events, awaited by everyone, were launched by the swimming competition. The participants had to swim from the river bank to the anchored ship, and the winner received a cash prize. Arriving on the ship, the over thirty amateur swimmers lined up on it, ready for the start of the duck catching competition. Ten domestic ducks were thrown ashore and after five seconds the competition was launched, the swimmers dived into the water and followed them, swimming and fighting to catch them. The caught ducks were the trophies of the competition.

The contest that lasted the longest, arousing the enthusiasm and fun of the hundreds of people gathered on the seafront, was the balance contest on the pole, whose much desired trophy was the piglet, over thirty kilograms, which hung above the water, well tied to the free end of the pole. This was a beam of beech, round and polished, seven or eight meters long, fixed horizontally, with one end firmly attached to the ship, and the other above the water, three or four meters high. In order to make the difficulty and fun even greater, the pole had been well greased with vaseline, so the competitors fell into the water after only two or three steps and hilarious attempts to keep their balance, to the cheers and laughter of the audience on the shore. The winner of the competition, the first to reach the struggling and frightened piglet, was designated after about forty minutes, enough time for four or five attempts each and only after the vaseline was almost cleared from the pole.

After the swimmers went on their way and the spectators headed home or retreated in the rescuing shade of the trees in the park, the captain's ship was also towed to anchor.

There were only a few people left on the seafront, including the boys from Miraveda, to watch the few men fishing near the Pescăruș restaurant, where the water from the Grand Canal flowed into the arm of the Great River, which passed by the City, the other arm being over eight miles away.

At one point, a boy swimming about forty yards from the shore, probably coming from the other shore, taken and drained by the strong current of the water, began to cry desperately for help. The Great River took its toll every year, with at least three or four people drowning, most of them inexperienced swimmers trying to cross it. There were many terrifying stories circulating in the area with swimmers who, having cramps or being caught in a deadly vortex, perished in the dark depths of the Great River.

Moreover, there were stories that paralyzed even the strongest and most experienced swimmers with fear, about the occasional rescuers, who were grabbed in the arms by desperate victims, drowning together and being found trapped, even after a few days, in the relentless arms of death.

A young man ran immediately down the river, taking off his shirt, and after overtaking the boy in the water by about twenty meters, taking off his pants, he plunged into the water. Elaur and his friends ran in the same direction, looking at the sinewy man, who was swimming swiftly towards the boy who had begun to swallow water, reaching him after he had disappeared under the water and catching him just as he came to the surface again. He placed him on his back, swimming in the breaststroke style, slowly approaching the shore, the water of the river carrying them downstream, for which reason, those on the shore, who were more and more, gathered from the park and were also moving in the same direction, encouraging the swimmer who was also moving harder and harder.

Terrified, first by the relentless presence of death, now that the two had a little to the shore, helped by another boy, who had also jumped into the water, Elaur was even more terrified to discover that the savior was none other than the grumpy and murderous Codrus. He didn't understand how he was free, thinking that maybe he had escaped from prison, from the desire to take revenge on someone, maybe even him. As the people on the shore began to applaud the savior, Elaur retreated behind them, whispering to Lefan:

"Let's get the hell out of here! Can't you see that this savior is Codrus, the murderer from Strugurelu?"

Seeing that Lefan, who did not know about his affair with Codrus, when he had put the knife at his neck on the night of the murder, as well as the other boys from Miraveda did not intend to follow him, he said to them:

"I'm leaving! I'll wait for you at the confectioner's!"

He bought a juice and sat down at an indoor table, although the few existing customers at that time sat on the outdoor terrace. He watched, through the large window of the confectioner's, the exit from the park, waiting for Lefan and the other boys from Miraveda to appear and fearing that Codrus might appear first. He did not understand how Codrus was free after less than two years, when everyone knew that he had been sentenced to twenty-five years in prison. The boys appeared after a quarter of an hour, only Lefan entering the confectionery.

"You'll be surprised, but there's no need to be afraid. Vali will tell you exactly what happened, because his grandmother is a cousin of Codrus' mother."

He came out carefully from the confectioner's, still staring fearfully at the cliff, and hurried toward the group of boys who were in front. When he caught up with them, Vali began to explain:

"My grandmother was at Codrus's house about a week ago, when he was released from prison, although she was a little afraid of him. Shortly after he arrived in quod, he was found unconscious in his cell and taken to the hospital. From there, they took him to the Capital, to that hospital, where they take the twisted guys! He got emergency surgery on his head and they took out, I don't know what, a piece of bone or something that had been pressing on his brain since that lawyer hit him with the car. Nobody knows how, but after the surgery he was completely changed. He is no longer violent and even his face has changed. You know he had that crooked mouth that could terrify you, only if he looked at you."

"Alright! He had surgery and he is no longer violent, but the punishment does not remain a punishment? I still don't understand how they let him go!"

"Apparently they took him to several doctors, studied him and after a year the trial reopened and they found him innocent, because that blow to the head would have changed his behavior. My grandmother told me that at the trial he was defended exactly by that lawyer from the City, who had knocked him down with his car."

"But you saw him now with your own eyes! It seems to me that he still has that face of a criminal, since I first saw him at school! And now, this is it? He's a changed man?"

"He seems changed to me. Look, ask Lefan too!"

"He seems changed to me as well, Lefan told him. You should have seen him smile that he saved that boy! He even stroked his face and reassured him! You can't even believe he's the same, because I knew the entire school was afraid of him!"

Elaur listened slightly puzzled, somehow reliving the horror he had gone through, but said nothing and preferred to change the subject. When he got home, he couldn't wait for the evening to come, to tell Gigi, the only one in the family who knew his secret and who upset him quite a lot, when he answered, calmly:

"Oh, well, I knew it, but I didn't want to tell you they let him go. I thought it was better you didn't know!"

Elaur looked at him in astonishment and said:

"Do you know what you're talking about? What do you mean, it would have been better? What if I met him face to face? Couldn't I have gone crazy? At least now I know he's not violent anymore!"

The fact that he had found out all those things did not save Elaur, the next night, from a new nightmare, in which a stranger pushed him with his head under the river water, waking up at about four o'clock, scared and breathing hard, unable to fall asleep until it was light. He kept thinking, until morning, about Codrus and what could be in his mind, when he remembers the one he killed.

Chapter 20

In just two days, after a rain that had come as a salvation over Miraveda, burnt by heat and drought, Elaur awoke in the morning, as the sky was covered with white clouds. The clean and refreshing air almost reflexively reminded him of the paradise of their childhood, the plot in the valley. He picked up a book from the high school library and went to the high shore, where he knew the cool air felt best, especially since the light wind was blowing from the Great River. On the road he remembered very clearly the words of his mysterious friend, Tinu, who had said more than a year and a half before, after Codrus was arrested: "You don't have to be afraid anymore! His anger will go as it came!" Besides that, his hope of meeting him again was fulfilled.

"Hello, Mr. Tinu! I am very happy to meet you again! I have so many things to tell you!"

He sat down next to him, on the grass that was burnt by the summer heat. He told him about the high school admission exam, what extraordinary teachers he had, his intentions to attend the humanities department and then the Faculty of Letters in the Capital.

"Elaur, I'm so happy for you! Be glad because you can study everything you want! The whole world is open to you and you can continue your studies, according to your heart and mind. I feel that many beautiful and interesting things are waiting for you, to discover and learn them, then to teach others, even if the education system will not be part of your life!"

Then he told him the story on the cliff, with Codrus rescuing the boy from drowning and everything he had learned about him and his brain surgery. Tinu nodded slowly and said:

"God listened to his mother's ardent prayers! Only the power of the Lord is greater than the power of a mother's prayer!"

"But the damage done by Codrus can no longer be repaired! The man killed by him lies in the grave and his children grow up without a father! His atonement will endure his entire life! Today he was not by the river by chance! And then, who are we to judge? We fulfill our destiny and if we can do well, we must do it! This and nothing more!"

They were both silent for two or three minutes, after which Tinu, feeling the unstoppable whirlwind of thoughts in Elaur's mind, but also the strong and contradictory feelings that were a burden on his soul, continued:

"My dear Elaur, good and evil have the same mother, and their mother is the mind of man! Evil grows everywhere, like a weed that cannot be eradicated, because it pairs well with stupidity, but it's even worse when it pairs with intelligence and they become the parents of cunning, which is the constant evil!"

Elaur listened intently, trying to penetrate the deepest parts of his friend's words, thinking that his lack of sight protected him from the lust of the eyes, but also from the brightness of lies, covered with gold and gems.

"When you do harm, it's like holding a venomous snake by the tail. You turn him against whoever you want, but the snake will turn on you!"

Tinu's words, which had something of the gentleness of the words of a gifted priest, but also of the dark mystery of the words of an old fortune teller, awakened in Elaur's mind and soul not only ideas and feelings, but also indelible images.

"When the evil comes to you, lock it in the dungeons of the mind, do not let it spread in the world, because it will return to you strengthened! Too many people complain about the evil that strikes them, without even understanding that most of the time, they brought it into the world themselves and now it's turning on them, like a drunken and loser son, ready to shatter their wealth and sometimes even their life."

He continued after a few moments of silence:

"I don't want to fill your head! Many, too many things, we learn only through suffering, but one thing remains for you at least, from the blind Tinu, the one who has never seen the light! The evil you do to anyone poisons you first and only good heals you. The good you spread in the world will return sooner or later to you, to enlighten your life, like a loving son!"

Elaur looked at Tinu, extremely concentrated, and the latter, though he could not see, knew this all too well, being very proud of his younger friend. Eventually, Elaur, after taking Tinu to his gate, left for home, excited and impressed, as if he had read an impressive book written by an author who had appeared out of nowhere.

The second year of high school began with other surprises and worries for Elaur. In the humanities department he found himself the only boy in a class of girls, half of whom were former colleagues of his, from the first year. In addition, he had been very sad to learn that his great passion, Miss Roza, the beautiful and refined French teacher, had transferred to a famous high school in the Capital. She left behind so many admirers, but also some colleagues who were happy that they had escaped "such a crazy woman", at the second examination in the summer. Being in the same class with Geta, his colleague, who had finished the first year with a higher gpa than his, intelligent and extremely ambitious, at least he still had the chance of the competition, which he was always looking for, even if it was a bit tough, especially with boys, until it seemed unbearable.

A few days later, he was called to the teachers'room by a mathematics teacher of the same name as his friend from Miraveda, who had taught mathematics for two other classes in the first year. He showed up at the teachers' room, not too surprised, wondering what the teacher might have to do with him.

Dark-haired, with premature gray hair, which highlighted his olive skin even more, Professor Peter had one of the corners of his mouth less mobile than the other, following a small accident in childhood, which was especially noticeable when he spoke. At his suggestion, they went out into the quiet hallway, which led to the chemistry and physics laboratories, they sat at the window sill to discuss freely a topic Elaur had sensed.

"I studied your first year grades and came to the conclusion that you oscillate between your passion for literature and your skills for math."

Elaur listened, flattered and confused alike, waiting to see what else Professor Peter would say, looking at him relentlessly, his black eyes expressing intelligence as well as determination.

"Actually this is the topic of our conversation. I started a very important project for me, but especially for students with certain skills, to organize a special math class. I received approval from the Ministry of Education and I have twenty-eight students from the two theoretical high schools in the city, who met the conditions imposed by the ministry, to organize this special class. Unfortunately, the ego of the teachers from the other high school made four of the pupils who agreed to come to this project change their mind after our approval came. We need a minimum of twenty-five students, who have obtained in the first year over B in mathematics and the general grade and in physics over B minus. Now I am left with only twenty-four and only you and your colleague Geta still meet these conditions!"

Elaur listened intently to Professor Peter's presentation and felt he was very bitter about what had happened. He knew something from his friend Vior about this special class where, besides him and Peter, among the friends from Miraveda, there was also Arian, his former classmate, from middle school, but also another boy, Elu, who had finished in the eighth D class.

"I also talked to Geta. She told me she will think about it and in two days she will give me the answer. I want you both! It would be a shame to waste your proven math skills. The curriculum in the special class provides an almost double number of hours of mathematics, which substantially increases your chances of being admitted at a good college at the University, the Polytechnic or the Academy of Economic Studies."

Elaur looked at him rather confused, feeling that he could not betray his great love, literature.

"I've also talked to Mrs. Culia! I didn't expect her to agree and I understand her perfectly. Who would give up the best two pupils in the class? But now, it's not about teachers, it's about pupils. It's about their skills and the chance to succeed in life. She told me that you both opt for the Faculty of Letters, right?"

Elaur liked the teacher's last reasoning, but allowed himself to contradict him:

"Indeed, greater certainty of success is important, but for good results, in addition to skills, passion is also needed!"

"You're absolutely right, but I don't think you could've got such good marks in math without putting a little passion into it! And then, you know the saying, appetite comes with eating! Speaking of passion, after the Faculty of Letters, what do you want to do?"

"I am interested in journalism and literature!"

"I asked you on purpose, because my wife graduated from the Faculty of Letters. None of her colleagues who tried to work for the media was accepted. She dreamed of becoming a writer! She also wrote a few short stories. Do you know how much she published? Nothing! Out of an entire graduating class, only a few got to publish something, but don't ask what they live on!"

Elaur, dazed by the harsh information provided by the math teacher, who apparently knew what he was talking about, was in no hurry to give an answer, so Professor Peter continued:

"My wife received a government assignment, as a literature teacher, in a muddy village, thirty kilometers from the city, and for four years she commuted daily, until a tenured position was opened here, with eleven candidates. She won the competition and she was happy, even if the job was for middle school and not high school, as she wanted."

"Professor, thank you very much for this offer and for the information, but I also want to give you the answer in two days!"

"I agree! But remember, with your soul you choose what is for the soul. School is more for the mind, so choose with your mind! Then literature can remain a beautiful passion!"

In order to better understand what is with this math special, he went straight to that class, looking for his friends from Miraveda. After entering the classroom, until he reached the desk of one of them, Cora, Geta's former first-year classmate, came to him as well.

"I think I know why you came! Professor Petre contacted you, didn't he? I know he talked to Geta too!"

In addition to the four friends from Miraveda, he also greeted Iani, a first-year colleague, but also Mihu, the country boy with whom he had befriended at the admission, and his deskmate, Enea, a silent boy, always with a smile on his face, whom he knew from football so both of them smiled in a friendly way.

"Geta is in the hospital, Cora said, but tonight I'm going to talk to her and I think I'll convince her to come! I kept a place for her!"

Elaur felt not only attracted, but also provoked by the very high level of the class, in which he noticed, pleasantly surprised, other very pretty girls, whom he had seen in the halls of the high school, but also completely unknown figures, probably the boys transferred from the other high school.

He then recognized Victor, a boy who was so internalized that he seemed almost absent, and had surprised him with the modern lyric of his poems, published in the high school's "Trepte" (*The Steps*) magazine, but who had also chosen the special mathematics class. What Professor Peter was saying was still resonating in his ears, "Then literature can remain a beautiful passion", he even remembered a well-known abstract poet, who was at the same time a great mathematician.

After school he left for home quite confused, and decided in the five or six minutes, how long it took to get home, to remain in the humanities department and keep his love for literature, the departure to the science department seemed to him a betrayal in love.

The next day, after learning that Geta had already agreed to transfer to the special math class, he went home, by chance, behind the four friends from Miraveda, who were talking passionately about a geometry of space problem. Encouraged by the conversation with his colleagues, Peter kept his arm free, in a ridiculous position, suggesting the position of a straight line, in an imaginary parallelepiped, which the other three even saw in their mind's eye. He felt immediately that a great loss was about to occur, if he would leave his group of friends, and as the competition with Geta was lost, from an almost uncontrollable impulse, but also to burn the return bridges, he entered in the middle of the group of friends and decreed:

"You'll have a new classmate from Miraveda starting from tomorrow!"

Their outburst of joy was in unison, they all congratulated him in turn, and Arian, his rival from middle school, added happily:

"Haven't I told you yesterday that Elaur will be my deskmate?"

From the first year, Elaur kept thinking about Lexia, his mysterious friend, and hoped to meet her again. Time passed and although he was always looking for her in the high school library, on the road that crossed Miraveda, on the streets of the City and even on the alleys of the Great Park, Lexia refused to appear. One evening, as he was walking toward the City center, he thought he recognized her, walking in front of him. He hurried to catch her, as the dress of the girl in front of him was as elegant and sophisticated as Lexia's special outfits.

He almost even approached her when he noticed that she was a pretty girl, who looked like Lexia, but to his great disappointment, it wasn't her. In May, on the pretext of looking for a book he needed in literature classes and which he could not find, he went to the school in Miraveda, to the librarian Alicia, who remembered him very well, and was happy to see him again. After explaining to her how much he needed the book, which was not even part of a middle school library's book collection, the author being studied only in high school, Elaur built up the courage and asked about Lexia:

"Miss Alicia, I met a girl here at the library, Lexia, who is older than me and who dresses very nicely, do you know where I can find her?"

The librarian told him that she did not know her, but she seemed more and more confused by the details provided by Elaur, as if he had told her about an alien. Elaur, knowing the secret of Miss Alicia, who from time to time had a bizarre behavior, with which she had even scared the teachers, but especially the school management, went home bitterly.

After three or four weeks spent in the special math class, Elaur was not yet used to Professor Peter's exaggerated pretensions. All the time he had to solve many complicated math problems, including those from the national magazine, The Mathematics Journal. He missed his compositions for literature classes, but also his endless readings, thinking more and more about Lexia, the girl who had vanished without a trace, longing for the conversations he had with her.

After mid-October, as the weather was still quite beautiful, on a Sunday afternoon, after several math problems solved, attracted by the gentle sun that illuminated their yard, he went to the shore at the edge of the nearby plot, firmly convinced that Tinu was already there. Indeed, as soon as he arrived, he saw his familiar figure.

"Long live Mr. Tinu! I really hoped to meet you, because I want to discuss more issues with you!"

He began to tell him about his transfer to a special math class, talking about his new plans for the future, thinking he would probably choose a college at the Polytechnic in the Capital. Towards the end, he moved on to the problem that bothered him the most, Lexia's disappearance.

For such a delicate mission, Tinu took his right hand between his big palms and after Elaur put his left palm to his heart, he asked him to think about Lexia. Elaur looked intently at the increasingly puzzled face of his blind friend, hoping to get the information he needed to find his special friend. Tinu looked quite confused, his face was really concentrated, like when you try to understand a text that is too far away, but after less than a minute, it suddenly lit up and he said:

"Lexia doesn't exist! In fact, Lexia is all you, Elaur!"

THE END

www.ingramcontent.com/pod-product-compliance
Lightning Source LLC
LaVergne TN
LVHW091304150826
845673LV00006B/1535

* 9 7 8 6 3 0 3 1 2 0 5 8 4 *